Repairing Hearts in Summit County

Summit County Series, Book 5

Katherine Karrol

ISBN 9781099269783

Repairing Hearts in Summit County

Contents

Chapter 1

Bella took one last look around the bedroom. Her closet, once full of expensive, fashionable – *boring* – clothes, were empty, thanks to the designer consignment shop she'd found. The styling products that filled the shelves in the bathroom were staying, as was the hated straightening iron.

She caught her reflection in the bedroom mirror and her long, straightened-to-death black hair grabbed her attention. As she looked it over, she spoke in the most dramatic Texas drawl she could muster. "Well, that just won't do, Sugah."

She walked into the bathroom, grabbed a pair of scissors, and prepared to remake herself. Remembering what her favorite stylist from years gone by did once, she grinned as she bent over, brushed her hair straight out from the top of her head, twisted it, and cut. A little water on her hands running through it unleashed the natural curls, and she looked in the mirror with satisfaction.

"That's more like it. *That* is hair befitting our new life."

She thought about leaving what she cut off as a snarky parting gift for Harrison since he loved it so much, but decided to make good out of a bad situation and stuffed it into an envelope to donate.

Pausing, she looked heavenward. "Lord, I really need to get better at making a dramatic exit, don't I?"

When the date on the calendar caught her eye as she made the last sweep through the kitchen, she laughed out loud. There was something fitting about leaving on April Fools' Day. It felt symbolic, as she was leaving behind the world that had made her feel like one.

As she drove away from the big, cold house and away from her old, cold life, she put down the windows and found an 80's and 90's music station to blast. One more stop as she headed out of town, and she would be on her way.

The visit to the car dealership was quick, and she walked away with cash in hand and a fully paid off car that didn't make her look like a pretentious snob. *Who thought a Porsche sedan was a good idea, anyway? The same person who filled your closet with clothes you hated and your social calendar with people who made you want to run screaming into the woods.*

She purposely took the most scenic and inefficient route as she made her way from Texas to Michigan. It was a great transition time, and she drove as if she had all the time in the world. She alternated between freeways, where she could revel in the speed and let the wind run through her new above-the-shoulder hair, and two-lane highways through small towns, where she could walk around, have a tasty meal, and make conversation with real people. Staying in small motels that popped up every so often on the two-lane highways, eating at mom-and-pop diners, and creating a funky and unrefined new wardrobe out of findings from small resale stores helped her flip the switch from old to new life.

Even though Summit County was her destination and she had dreamed about returning there, she had no idea where it was other than that it was in Northern Michigan. "Thank You for Google, Lord. I wouldn't have known where to look on a map to find the place, and you know my parents never would have helped me. The only thing they want to help me with these days is moving back in with Harrison and continuing on as if nothing ever happened. Since they're barely speaking to me, I don't think they would be too keen on telling me how to find the place I've dreamed of returning to so I can start over."

She wiped a tear from her eye. "Please let this place be as great as I remember it, and help me to find a room or small apartment right away so I can get settled there." As she talked to God while she drove, she found that she had no shortage of words. At this moment in her life, she was more comfortable talking to Him than listening, but she told herself that when she got to her destination, she would close her mouth and open her ears.

Over the handful of days driving up through small towns and long stretches of tree-lined highways, she let the fresh air blow her old life off her. The last day of her trip required the windows to be up, but since she didn't need to freeze to death to feel free, it was okay. By that point, she was cleansed.

Her excitement grew as the navigation app told her she was approaching her destination. She had made a reservation at a little motel in Hideaway, a small town on Lake Michigan, and the woman who ran it sounded like the perfect hostess on the phone.

She hoped she liked the area as much as she remembered. Actually, she didn't remember much at all, but she had liked it enough to keep the picture of herself and her sister in front of the 'Welcome to Summit County' sign that was taken when she had been there as a child. That picture had been special enough that she had kept it in the memory box that traveled with her every time her family moved. She had vague memories of the cottage they had rented during that vacation, but distinct ones of how she felt there.

When she saw the sign that said "Hideaway 52 Miles" on the highway, she let out a little whoop.

"Fifty-two miles to my new life . . . maybe. Okay, fifty-two miles to, at the very least, my pit stop on the way to my new life." She looked toward heaven. "Lord, please make this my new life. Actually, no. I decided last time what my life was going to be, or at least I decided to let others decide and followed along. This time I want *You* to show me and make a life for me. I'm done ignoring Your voice, and we're in this together."

A knot started in her stomach when she looked at the navigation app and saw that she was thirteen miles out. *I hope I haven't gotten my hopes up over nothing.*

She took a couple of slow breaths. *It will be fine. Either you'll love it or you won't. Easy peasy. If you love it, you'll stay, and if you don't, you won't. This is a risk-free adventure.*

Even though it was brisk, she wanted to smell the fresh air that the trees were creating all around her. She turned up the heat in the car and put the windows down so she could smell her new world.

Everything looked fresh and *alive.* Many of the trees were evergreen, and the rest were full of new growth. It was strange to see the occasional patch of snow left over from the winter on the side of the road where the trees blocked the sun, but she supposed it was just one of many things that would be completely new and different for her. She hadn't given much thought to winter in northern Michigan, but she would cross that snowy bridge when she came to it. Her plan was to give herself six months to experiment with a new place and make a home, and she was determined not to get ahead of herself.

She had enough money budgeted for those six months, and if she could find work, it would stretch out longer. When she had deposited the settlement check from Harrison, she had immediately invested a large portion, started an IRA with another portion, put some in an emergency fund, and set aside six months of living expenses. She then took the longest, hottest, soapiest shower of her life to try to get rid of how dirty she felt taking what amounted to hush money.

Hush money or shrewd deal, it was funding her new life. It was giving her the opportunity to finally figure out what kind of life *she* wanted and to create it. Signing the agreement not to talk about Harrison's extramarital activities wasn't that difficult, actually. The last thing she wanted to talk about was the fact that her husband didn't find her or their marriage vows to be enough for him.

When the navigation app said two miles, Bella was so giddy that she had to use the cruise control to stay somewhere near the speed limit. She didn't want the first thing she did in her new town to have anything to do with giving the police job security.

Awe filled her as she took in every curve and tree on the road and absorbed the beauty. She passed a large inland lake on her right and wondered if it was the one she'd spent time at as a child. It looked familiar enough that she figured it must be. As she crested a hill, the sight took her breath away. Ahead were a few more large hills, then what she guessed must be Hideaway, and beyond that, Lake Michigan. The midday sun shining on the white caps on the waves made the contrast to the deep blue of the water a striking sight.

"I'm here!" She cranked the Hillsongs CD she'd been listening to up to full blast and danced around in her seat.

The final hill before entering the town was crowned with a large gateway welcoming travelers to Hideaway, and it felt as if she were entering a different world as she passed through it and the town below came into view. The charming Ferrytown Motel, where she'd made the reservation, was on the main road, but she wasn't ready to stop just yet. She continued to the end of the town where Lake Michigan waited. Even though the wind was strong and the waves looked fierce, it somehow calmed her soul. She sat and watched the waves crash over the breakwater for several minutes, and when she couldn't put off a bathroom break any longer, she headed back to the little motel. This area was definitely a place she could call home for the next six months while she and God decided what to do next.

Chapter 2

Mitch Huntley approached the Marvel Point lighthouse shortly after sunrise, ready to win. He was meeting Clay Cooper, one of his best friends and his most worthy opponent, for what might be the last snowshoeing race for the season. His mind needed the clearing that only pushing his physical limits would bring, and between the heavy snow and the competition, he would get it. The fact that whoever won the last race of the season got natural bragging rights for the summer was just a bonus.

He saw Clay's car, but no Clay. He looked around just as Clay climbed out of the passenger side door of Shelby Montaugh's car.

"Morning date?"

"Funny; morning chat with a friend who happened to be here to watch the sun rise."

Sure. The look on Clay's face suggested that he wished she was more than a friend, but when he had something to say about it, he would, and Mitch wasn't one to pry. They both waved to Shelby as she drove away with the same look on her face.

"You ready to lose a race?" Clay grinned at him and looked like he was about to start without him.

Mitch laughed. "I'm ready to humiliate you, if that's what you meant to say. The usual course?"

"Let's do it."

As always, the two were neck and neck the whole way. Mitch's muscles and lungs burned as they passed the downed branch that they used as the finish line. He raised his hands in victory and let out a howl.

"I let you win. You're welcome."

"You keep telling yourself that." The two old friends laughed as they caught their breath and headed toward their cars.

"Time for a quick breakfast?"

Mitch looked at his watch. "Sure. I'll probably be on my own again at work today, so I need to get over there early. Bay Shore Diner?"

"See you there."

The diner was mostly empty, which was typical for early April. As soon as they sat down, Clay asked how things were going.

"Good. Things are still a little slow at the store, but I'm stocking up for spring."

Clay arched his brow and cocked his head, reminding him that he wasn't making small talk. "I'll be more specific. How are you holding up?"

Mitch sighed and rubbed his face with his hands. "Okay. I get sleep when I can and I take every day in pieces."

"Is there anything I can do, other than pray for you and Zack? I'd like to help."

"I know you would, and you know that if there's anything you can do, I'll let you know."

Clay was one of the few people who knew what Mitch's life had been like for the last several months since his nephew Zack had returned from the front lines with a Purple Heart, a prosthetic leg, and Post-Traumatic Stress. Mitch wished there was something someone else could do to lighten the load on himself and his sister, but they were Zack's only lifelines at the moment.

"Has there been any word from the VA or that other place you told me about?"

"No, he's still on waiting lists at both places, so we're doing what we can here in the meantime. He's holding on okay, and some days are better than others."

"And you still don't know why it's been worse lately?"

He shook his head. "Not a clue. It seems like the rough spots go in waves for him, but we have no idea why. Every day I wake up hoping it's a good day and wait to see what happens. The last couple of nights were good with no texts or calls, so today started as a good day." He chuckled. "I even got enough rest last night to beat you this morning."

"I let you."

"Uh-huh."

Mitch wished Zack had a friend like Clay to help him with reentry. Mitch had gotten out of the Army shortly before Clay returned to Hideaway after college and a brief try at the NFL, cut short by a knee injury. It was great timing for both and the long friendship had deepened as they each avoided public places and licked their respective wounds. Neither talked much about what they were going through at first; they spent most of their time watching movies and playing cards. When Clay's knee and Mitch's nervous system healed enough, they got back to the sports and activities they both loved together. Eventually Clay's anger and Mitch's numbness wore off enough that they started talking about what their experiences had been like and helped each other get back on solid footing. Mitch was determined to give his nephew what he had and was ready to make any sacrifice in order to do so.

Chapter 3

Bella took it as a sign from above that the owner of the Ferrytown Motel happened to have a friend with an apartment over her detached garage that she was willing to rent out for the summer and that it was available immediately. It was also helpful with the budget, considering she only had to stay at the motel for two nights before finding out about it.

The tiny little apartment above the garage was perfect. The entire place was less square footage than the bedroom in her last house and there was no dishwasher, garbage disposal, wifi, or central air, but it was somehow still perfect.

"Did I mention that this place is perfect?" The Bluetooth in her ear made it easy to unpack and move things where she wanted them while she talked with her best friend, Dani.

"Yes, I think you said that one or a thousand times. I just don't get your fascination with something so basic if you're planning to spend the whole summer. I know you're worried about finances, but can't you at least get a small house or a condo that has a few amenities? It sounds adorable, but I'm just afraid the excitement is going to wear off and you're going to feel claustrophobic and miserable." Dani meant well, and she knew Bella better than anyone. She had been there through the best and worst of times since freshman year of college, but even she had no idea what Bella needed right this moment.

"Come and visit me! If you see it, you'll see why I love it and why it's so–"

"Perfect. I get it." She chuckled. "Maybe I can come for a visit once you get settled in. Do they have motels there? *Kidding*! Seriously, though, are you sure you're going to be okay? You know you don't have to do this. You can start over anywhere and you don't actually *have* to leave Dallas. You don't have anything to be ashamed of.

"As a matter of fact, you could come here to Colorado Springs to start over! Come on, Bella! You can stay with us for a few months while you get your bearings. It will be fun! I'll help you get to know the area and I'll introduce you to more people. You already know more people here than in the hundred-mile radius around – wait, what's it called again?"

"It's called Summit County. Stop acting like you don't know its name; you sound like a snob. I spent a lot of time thinking and praying about where I wanted to move, and as much as I love you and love visiting Colorado Springs, it's your place, not mine. I need to create something of my own. Dallas was Harrison's, and I never felt like it was home. I lived there for six years and never got comfortable. I've been here for a few days and I already feel my roots growing."

She smiled as she looked out the window. "There's just a feeling here. And if I'm sitting in the right spot in my tiny, perfect living room, I can watch the sun rise over the lake. This is a place I could live in forever."

"Okay, okay. I get it. It's perfect. Oh shoot! I just looked at the clock and I have to go pick Connor up. Do you want me to call you back when I get in the car?"

"No, you go do your stuff. I don't need to hear you telling other drivers what morons they are. We'll talk in a few days, okay?"

"Okay. Just give me an update on the job search. And send me pictures of your adorable little twelve-square-foot sanctuary so I can see what you do with the place."

She hung up the phone and continued unpacking the box in front of her. There was no way she was going to fit even the small amount of stuff she brought without it looking like an episode of Hoarders. *It's time to simplify.* She went about choosing the most vital kitchen tools and versatile pots and pans.

When she finally sat down, she was exhausted. *Who unpacks everything the day they move in? Only OCD people and people who have a tiny bit of space in a perfect garage apartment that they're determined to make a home, apparently.*

She thought back to the last time she moved into a new home – well, a house. It was definitely not a home, but not for lack of trying. She should have had a graduate degree with all the home decorating shows she watched. She discovered that she enjoyed making things homey, but even making places homey didn't make them homes. Harrison was willing to let her do what she wanted in the parts of the home that weren't used for entertaining, but it was always in the context of *letting* her do what she wanted in *his* house. He said it was their home, but that was simply a facade. The house aptly mirrored the relationship inside it.

"Lord, thank You for my beautiful, perfect little apartment. Thank You for the beautiful wood walls and floors and for the cool latches on the doors and for the little creaks. Show me how to make it mine. Actually, show me what it's like to *have* a home."

Chapter 4

Mitch took one last walk through the store before locking up and heading home. There was something calming about seeing everything in its place and from the time he had bought the store from his father, he had made a ritual of strolling the tidy aisles as he ended his day. It took him back to the childhood spent playing on those floors and watching his father help people and serve his community and it gave him a sense of order.

He was glad the next shipments of gardening supplies and deck stains had arrived that afternoon. Staying busy made the days of working alone go by much faster, and tedious jobs like unpacking boxes and setting up displays were good ways to spend the days after getting minimal sleep.

As he walked to his truck, he sent a quick text to Zack reminding him that he was taking the texts and calls again for the night and wished him a good night's sleep. His own sleep would start as soon as he got home in case it would be like the night before and he would spend hours on the phone with Zack in the middle of it.

He was fast getting back into the swing of surviving on a few hours of sleep at a time. In the eight years since his discharge from the Army, he'd forgotten some of his skills for surviving on constant alert; now that Zack needed him, they were all coming back.

Zack was his nephew, but had always been more like a little brother to him, thanks to the mere seven-year age difference between them. There was less of an age difference between Mitch and Zack than between Mitch and his own siblings. He was a late-in-life baby for his parents, and his sisters treated him more like their living doll than a brother when he was little. Long before his parents retired and moved to Florida, they were less able to attend every sport and activity Mitch was involved in, and his sisters took over as stand-ins, especially Cynthia, Mitch's oldest sister and Zack's mother.

Cynthia had sacrificed so much of her social life, finances, and life plans for Mitch when he was younger that he would do anything for her and her son. Zack's father had thankfully left the picture years before, so Cynthia had the role of both parents. It took some time for Mitch to convince her to let him share the load with Zack since he'd returned home, but she had finally relented and they had figured out a good system and schedule. It helped that Zack had taken the job Mitch offered at the hardware store soon after his return; Mitch could keep an eye on him and Zack had an understanding boss.

Chapter 5

Bella settled into the overstuffed chair that she'd positioned to maximize the view of Sapphire Lake. Looking at the beautiful scene seemed to make her morning coffee taste extra delicious as she sipped it, and she'd delighted in the view every morning as if it was the first one. The crystal clear water with its various shades of blue was fast becoming her favorite sight and brought a smile to her face instantly. The leaves on the trees had popped over the previous day as Spring sprang forward, and she took a few moments to just stare and thank God for creating such a beautiful world. It was still a little cool to have the window open, but she couldn't resist. She opened it just a crack so that she could smell the fresh air and tucked her blanket around herself more securely.

She told herself that once she got settled in to the new place, she would get back to her morning routine from long ago of reading her Bible and journaling in the mornings, but she wasn't quite settled enough for that yet. She was still having a hard time focusing enough to read her Bible, but it felt comforting to just hold the big, weathered book. She knew God was there with her and was comforting her in the midst of what she was going through, and she could still hear His voice, even if she rarely stilled herself enough to just listen.

For a time, she clutched her Bible and stared at the lake. She read a chapter in Proverbs, chastised herself for picking the low hanging fruit of an easy book, reminded herself that reading a short, easy passage was still reading Scripture, and thought about journaling. *Maybe later. There's too much to do right now.*

A part of her knew that the voice in her head that accused her of not being a good enough wife to keep her husband from straying and of not having enough faith to make the marriage work might be wrong, but she couldn't quite shake the fear that she was a disappointment to God. She couldn't bear hearing it directly from Him, so she was just going to have to keep busying herself for the time being, and keep her conversations with Him more on the small talk end of the spectrum.

She looked at the usual job posting and networking sites, followed a couple of leads down rabbit holes that proved useless, and thanked God for the fund that allowed her time to find the next job. Another job in marketing wasn't even something she was sure she wanted. What was once fun and exciting had become a chore, just like everything else in life had. She could sleepwalk through a marketing campaign and often *had* in recent months; still, it was what she knew and did well. She thought about making a website for online consulting and jotted down a few ideas about both the website and the prospective clients she wanted to attract. After a couple of hours, she admitted that it made her feel bored and dry and decided to go get to know her new area.

It hadn't taken long to explore Lakes End, the town that sat at the end of Sapphire Lake, the day before, as the entire town consisted of two short blocks, and she decided to venture into Hideaway, the town she had spent her first nights in and that was just a few miles in the other direction from her tiny little perfect apartment.

Chapter 6

Mitch was trying to stay awake after the third sleep-deficient night in a row. The pot of coffee he'd finished off was keeping him upright, but it was a struggle. The latest string of late-night conversations with Zack had finally taken a toll on him, and he was in no state for any high-level brain work or customer service or any extra hassles.

He looked at the clock again and sighed. It was only midway through the afternoon and he still had several hours to get through before he would have a chance for sleep.

When he saw an unfamiliar-looking woman wander in out of the corner of his eye, he figured it would be best to make himself scarce and found some shelves to rearrange on the other side of the store. It was unlike him to avoid customers, especially people who looked to be new in town, but today he had no capacity for such things; he was doing her a favor, really. He just wanted to get through the day, then go home and get some sleep.

There was a good chance that Zack would need him again in the wee hours of the morning and he had to be prepared. He was looking for tasks that would allow him to be busy but wouldn't require too much brain power or fine motor coordination and had just started moving around some camping equipment when he heard a crash from the other side of the store.

Reflex kicked in and he sprang into action. When he came around the corner and saw that the woman was upright but that she had sent the contents of the garden display he'd spent hours building and setting up the day before spilling and rolling down the aisle, his concern turned to irritation. *This is gonna be a long day.*

Chapter 7

U gh. How embarrassing. Less than a week into living here and I've become the Town Klutz already.

She crouched to pick up the items from the display that had scattered far and wide and hoped no one heard the commotion. She had started putting things back as they were when she heard a deep voice behind her.

"You can just put those everywhere."

Thinking he was joking, she started to giggle, but then winced when she turned and saw the storms in the man's eyes. The way he stood towering over her with his arms crossed, he looked like a brick wall, and she was sure she could see actual smoke coming out of his ears.

"I'm so sorry; I was focused on finding some wall hooks and backed right into this."

He let out a sigh. "It's fine. I'll take care of it."

The tone in his voice and look on his face suggested he was not at all interested in either her assistance or her witty banter. She slowly backed out of the store and didn't realize she'd stopped breathing until she was half a block away.

A little less attitude and a little more charm, and he could be cute. Not that I'm looking for cute. Or charming. Or a man. Or anything. She'd been with cute and charming, even married it, and that had turned out horribly. Six years down the road, with nothing but loneliness and heartache to show for it, she was starting life over in a new town in a new state far, far away from the life she'd tried her hardest to make the best of, and failed miserably.

Chapter 8

Mitch toyed with the idea of closing early so he didn't have to deal with any more customers turning his store into a demolition zone or take the risk of chasing more away. He was haunted both by the shock in the woman's eyes when she saw him standing over her a few minutes before and the teasing glint it had replaced, and was ashamed and embarrassed for acting like that. He was about to lock the door to protect any other potential victims of his mood when Joe Callahan walked in to pick up a pair of light fixtures he'd ordered for a renovation job he was working on.

"Yikes, looks like you had another rough night."

"I can barely keep my eyes open and I was just incredibly rude to a customer."

Joe winced. "That's definitely unlike you to be rude, especially to a customer. Why don't you go in the back and take a nap? I'm ahead of schedule at the Westons and can cover you for a couple of hours at least."

He looked around the store and sighed; he didn't even have the energy to protest. "I'll take you up on that offer. Don't worry about that display; I'll take care of it later. If I'm not back out here or Zack doesn't come in by the time you need to leave, just lock the front door, okay?" He rubbed his heavy eyes. "And if the beautiful but clumsy customer comes back in, apologize for me and remind yourself that you're engaged."

Joe grinned like a lovesick puppy. "Oh, there will be no need to remind myself of that. Maybe if it gets busy in here, I'll be able to get my mind off the fact that I still have to wait twenty-six more days to marry Emily."

Mitch chuckled as he started toward the back room. "You can do it, buddy."

He smiled at his friend's impatience and excitement. He had begun to wonder if Joe even had the ability to smile anymore over anything but his toddler daughter. He had been widowed on the day Lily was born and had thrown himself into fatherhood and making a life so great for her that she wouldn't miss having a mother. When Emily moved into town in the fall, Joe came back to life. Now Joe and Lily were a few weeks away from being part of a complete family again.

He was relieved to have the chance to catch some shut-eye. Not only was Zack having worse nightmares and insomnia lately, he was having a hard time working his shifts at the hardware store. Working alone most days and taking middle of the night texts and phone calls was wearing on Mitch.

It didn't take much time for him to fall asleep. He had learned how to go to sleep quickly and in less-than-ideal conditions in the Army, and the cot in the back room served its purpose just fine.

As he woke, he looked around the darkened room and grabbed his phone. He was surprised to find that he had slept for over three hours and was thankful both for the reprieve and for the fact that he hadn't missed anything from Zack. He sent him a text to check in and when Zack responded that he was doing okay, he breathed a sigh of relief. Cynthia was doing well when he checked in with her, too.

He thought about his own return from Afghanistan and wished for the thousandth time that he could trade experiences with his nephew. He had a hard time on reentry, but being hypervigilant and numb didn't compare to what Zack was going through. At least Mitch didn't have flashbacks or a prosthesis.

He walked out into the quiet store. Joe had left a note of apology for having to leave to pick Lily up before Mitch woke up. He had also left a detailed log of sales and cleaned up the display mess. Mitch told himself he was just being a responsible business owner when he looked in the log to see if anyone had bought wall hooks while he was sleeping.

Chapter 9

Bella didn't realize until hours after she'd left the hardware store that she'd forgotten to get the wall hooks she'd gone in there for in the first place. Not wanting to face the wrath of the man working there again, she decided to make do without them for the time being, at least until someone else was working. She had explored the few shops that were open in Hideaway and gotten lunch in the deli and was happy to find that the rest of the retail workers in Hideaway were quite friendly. She'd never been in a town that had seasonal shops and restaurants, and it just added to the charm of the place.

As she drove back toward the apartment, she took in the large trees lining the highway. Once she crested one of the hills, she could see Sapphire Lake beyond them. "Ooh, I think this just became my favorite view."

She wondered if anyone ever got tired of the scenery in the area and quickly decided that would be impossible. When she drove a good mile or two without seeing another car on the two-lane highway, she laughed out loud at the comparison to Dallas and Chicago and Atlanta and all the other cities she'd lived in.

"Yes, this place is perfect."

Growing up in metropolitan areas, she had always felt out-of-place. She never seemed to fit in with the fast pace and chaos, let alone the country clubs and parties she was always dragged to while her parents made contacts to further her father's career. She felt completely different on the rare occasions that her family took vacations in small towns filled with real people and she had always fantasized about staying in one of them.

When her life imploded and she had no hometown to return to, she decided to go back to the one place she knew the name of: Summit County. She didn't even remember where they had rented a house, but Sapphire Lake looked familiar when she drove past it upon her arrival to the area. When she heard about the apartment that had a view of it, she snatched it up.

She didn't know or care what she would do at the end of the summer, but for the time being, Summit County was the place she would see about calling home. If she decided to stay at the end of the summer, she would figure out what home really meant and how to create it.

Chapter 10

Thunder rumbled and lightning flashed as the storm hurtled across the lake and landed in Hideaway. Mitch had just poured a cup of coffee for himself and one for Zack when a gust of wind came through and the power went out.

Zack started heading for the back room. "I'll get the generator started."

"Thanks. I'll turn the surge protectors off in case this is like last time. Can you turn on the battery-powered sign up front on your way?"

"Sure."

Spring storms and power outages were nothing new or noteworthy in Northern Michigan, but Mitch never quite knew how Zack would respond when something caused a loud noise or change in lighting. Thankfully, today was a good day for Zack, and he was handling it calmly so far.

Zack was a hard worker and was always ready to go the extra mile on his good days. On his bad days, he couldn't get out of bed or come in at all. When he came around the corner hauling generators on the dolly, Mitch looked up and laughed.

"Remind me to give you a bonus next time there's extra cash in the account."

"Just trying to be ready for the rush on these; you know there will be one." Mitch began clearing an area in the corner so they could unload them.

"You've got a good business mind, Zack. Keep it up and I'll give you a promotion, too."

"I'm already Assistant Manager."

"Assistant *to the* Manager." There was never a bad time for a joke from *The Office,* and Mitch was glad that Zack was keeping both his bearings and sense of humor about him so far. Making certain jokes and gauging Zack's response was an amazingly accurate system for checking on Zack's mental state and Mitch used it often.

The wind howled outside as the storm hovered over. The rain came in at a sharp angle and Mitch kept watch out of the corner of his eye for any changes in Zack. With the generators ready and waiting for customers, he was calmly checking the radar on his weather app and wasn't showing signs of distress so far. When Cynthia darted into the store, Mitch gave her a subtle reassuring nod as she took off her soaking wet jacket.

"That is one cold rain! I was down the street and figured this would be a good place to hunker down until it passes."

"Can I get you some coffee, Mom?"

"Sure, honey. That sounds great."

As Zack went into the back room to get a cup for her, Mitch's text alert sounded. "No surprise there. The fire department is calling up the volunteers. I've got to go."

"I figured they would and hoped I would get here before you had to go."

"Your timing was perfect, sis. He's having a good day today and hasn't been reacting much to the storm, but text me if you need me."

He was glad that he and Cynthia had worked out a system for

days like this, too. As far as he could tell, Zack hadn't caught on to her 'coincidental' visits to the hardware store at times when he might get triggered and Mitch might get called away.

"Be careful."

"Always."

Chapter 11

Bella looked around the apartment and wondered where to take shelter if the need arose. Even though the storm didn't seem dangerous at the moment, she didn't know how bad storms got in her new home, and she'd lived in enough places that had dangerous tornadoes that she knew to scout out a spot in case it became necessary.

Her phone rang and she saw that it was her new landlady. "Hi, Mrs. Pullman. Are you okay?"

She chuckled. "I'm fine. It's just a little rain. I was calling to invite you to ride out the storm in the house with me. There is a fire roaring in the fireplace and a fresh pot of coffee brewing in the kitchen."

"I'm on my way."

The storm raged on and Bella was glad that Mrs. Pullman had a basement if they would need it. As they sat in front of the fire, Bella jumped every time she heard the thunder and lightning outside.

"Don't worry. The lake echoes the sound of the storm, so it makes it sound worse than it is." She looked out the window at the lake that looked as grey as the sky above it. "We don't have as many tornadoes around here as you had in Texas. The bigger threat around here is these old, tall trees. Every now and then they take out the power lines and block the roads."

No sooner had she said it than the room went dark. They laughed together as Bella joked, "And it was dark."

They got the generator running quickly and went back to their coffee in front of the fireplace.

"It's a good thing you made the coffee before the power went out."

"It's also a good thing that I have a gas stove and plenty of firewood. Why don't you stay for dinner and tell me more about yourself? Thunderstorms always put me in the mood for a nice, hearty soup."

"Dinner sounds great, but only if I can help with it."

It was nice chopping and talking while the storm continued outside. Storms that didn't threaten to turn into tornadoes were always comforting to Bella and she enjoyed the background noise the rain and wind provided.

"How long have you lived here, Mrs. Pullman?"

"I'll tell you all about it if you will stop calling me that. It's Nancy, remember?"

"Sorry. Growing up, it was 'Mr. and Mrs.' or there was a consequence. Old habits die hard."

"Well, we don't stand on formality around here. Where is your family now?"

Bella tried to sound casual. She didn't need Nancy to think she hauled a bunch of baggage around. "My parents live in Albuquerque right now, and my sister and her husband are in Boston."

"And you just came from Dallas but don't have an accent. Where is home to you?"

Bella thanked God that the question came when she was chopping onions and she had an excuse for not having dry eyes. "I never spent enough time in one place to have a hometown. My father is a corporate consultant, so he is hired to help businesses get out of financial trouble. The longest we were ever in one place was three years, and that was the exception."

She was glad that people didn't always realize that 'corporate consultant' was sometimes described as 'hatchet man' in her father's case. She hated being associated in any way with the person who saved companies and grew his own bank account by cutting jobs and pensions.

"My father was in the Army, so I know what all that moving is like. When I married my husband and we moved here, one of the most wonderful things was being able to go years without packing more than a suitcase for a trip."

Bella chuckled. "I would like to know what that's like. The good thing about moving a lot is that I don't cling to many possessions, and moving is easy." *The bad thing is that I have no idea what it's like to have a home.*

"Maybe you'll decide that you like this area and stay here."

"I'm hoping so. I would love to be able to put down roots somewhere."

Nancy had such a welcoming way about her. Bella wasn't used to people being so friendly and generous without ulterior motives, and reminded herself to just enjoy it.

It was nice making and then eating the soup together, and Bella enjoyed getting to know Nancy more. She even felt comfortable enough to give her the very short version of what led to her leaving Dallas and what brought her to the area. Just as they dried the last dish, they heard a loud cracking sound followed by a crash and felt the ground shake.

It was too dark to see where the tree fell, but obvious that it was close . . . and that it had hit a structure.

Chapter 12

Mitch fell into bed, exhausted and glad that Cynthia had insisted on taking Zack duty for the night. After spending hours helping clear large branches from the roads around Hideaway, he was sore and in desperate need of sleep. The storm didn't appear to cause any major damage, but the downed trees created the usual nuisance. He set his alarm just in case he needed it so he could open the store early. Those generators would likely fly off the shelves in the morning like they always did the day after a storm, and he was glad that Zack had put in an order for more while he was gone.

Fortunately, the storm had only lasted for a few hours. According to Cynthia, Zack had gotten more jumpy as it went on, but had kept himself busy at the store. It was likely that the storm would get Zack's anxiety ramped up, and Mitch again wished there was more he could do to help him.

When he had returned from Afghanistan, he'd had difficulty with crowds, sudden motion in his periphery, and sleep, but didn't have any of the degree of struggles Zack was having. Of course, his experience hadn't been as harrowing as Zack's, either. Mitch's second deployment was rough on him and he had lost friends, but never in front of him and never guys he was close with.

Mitch was again thankful for Clay and was determined to be as helpful to Zack as Clay had been to him. He wished he could pass on the faith to Zack that Clay had demonstrated to him, but he was still not too sure about how the whole leaning-on-God thing worked. Clay and Joe and other friends did and got a lot of strength from their faith, but he wasn't sure how to do it for himself. Though he had always believed, the idea of trusting God to take care of him and the people around him was one he had a hard time grasping. He was used to taking care of things himself, and wasn't sure how to let God share the load with him, let alone take it. He made a mental note to dig out the Bible Clay had given him and start reading soon. Maybe that would help him figure it all out.

Chapter 13

Bella woke in the strange bedroom and took a few moments to figure out where she was and why. *Storm . . . tree . . . big hole. My perfect little apartment got hit by a tree.*

Fortunately the damage didn't seem too severe, but her perfect little refuge was going to need some work. Nancy was shaken, but said she knew someone who could fix the damage and restore the interior so it would look like nothing had ever happened.

Bella hoped it could be fixed quickly and that she wouldn't have to move out while the work was being done. Nancy had assured her that it would be no problem for her to stay in the house while the apartment was being worked on, but Bella didn't want to inconvenience her – or to miss out on one day in the tiny garage sanctuary. She had only been there for a week and hated having to leave it.

When Nancy returned from her book club in Hideaway, she looked relieved. "We're all set. Joe Callahan will come over today and take a look at the damage to see what he can do to help. You'll like him; he's a wonderful young man, about your age."

Just as Bella was afraid Nancy was trying to play matchmaker, she continued, "He has a sweet fiancée who hasn't lived here long, either. I'll be sure to introduce you to her; I have a feeling the two of you will get along fabulously. They're getting married in a few weeks, so Joe is not sure if he will be able to finish the job before he goes on his honeymoon, but he guaranteed me that he'll do what needs to be done so it's safe for you and protected from water damage before he leaves."

Getting married. Not a setup. Cupid's bullet dodged. She breathed a sigh of relief, both for the apartment getting fixed soon and for avoiding a setup. She had absolutely no interest in getting involved with anyone anytime soon.

$$\infty\infty\infty$$

Bella held her breath while Joe surveyed the damage a few hours later. He looked like he knew what he was doing, but she wasn't sure if a local fix-it guy would be up to the task if it was going to be fully restored to the charm it had 24 hours before. *Stop being a big-city snob and see what happens. It's not your house, anyway.* Nancy looked completely confident in his ability to get the job done, and it was her home.

"I can get this roof and wall patched within the next couple of days, but I'm going to need some help with the plumbing because those pipes took quite a beating. I'll call Mitch and see when he can look at them. We're going to have to keep the water and electricity off until he checks it to make sure it's safe, but I'm sure he'll get here as soon as he can."

"That's just perfect. Thank you, Joe." Nancy looked reassured and Bella prayed that the plumber could get there soon so she could get out of Nancy's hair and back to her new life.

Chapter 14

Mitch groaned as he climbed out of bed. Zack had done fine during the storm two days before, but it had ramped up the nightmares and insomnia, which meant that Mitch hadn't gotten much sleep for the past two nights. It took everything in him to do some tasks and get through the day. He took as hot a shower as he could tolerate to loosen up his sore muscles and help him wake up, and made his way over to the store.

The customers were steadily coming in for the usual after-storm supplies, mostly generators, saws, and tarps, and staying busy was helping him stay awake. He wasn't sure how long he would be able to manage without hiring someone else to help out on the days that Zack couldn't, but he was determined to try to ride it out.

Joe stopped in to the store and Mitch was happy to see the large coffee he brought with him as well as the carry-out bag from the Bay Shore Diner.

"I brought you some sustenance. Nancy Pullman's renter asked again if you might be getting over there soon."

Mitch slapped his hand to his head. "I can't believe I forgot to get over there. I'll close the store and head over in a couple of hours when the traffic clears in here."

He hated forgetting things and hated letting people down. His brain was functioning on its lowest, most basic gear, and it was frustrating him to no end.

"You've been busy, and from the looks of you, still not getting any sleep. Have some lunch and I'll see if Emily can watch the store so you can ride over there with me."

"Thanks, man."

Mitch hated accepting help. He hated *needing* help. He was always much more comfortable in the position of help*er* than help*ee*, but had no choice in the matter. There weren't many people Mitch would feel comfortable leaving the store with, but Emily knew her way around tools, thanks to years of working on home renovation shows before moving to Hideaway. She also did bookkeeping and accounting work for him from time to time, so he trusted her and she knew the inventory of the store as well as he and Zack did.

∞∞∞∞

When they pulled up to Nancy's garage and walked toward the apartment, Mitch was prepared to grovel and offer his most heartfelt apology to the renter. He was also prepared to take his tardiness in getting started into consideration as he added up the bill for his services. Joe made a stop at Nancy's house while Mitch went straight to the apartment.

When the renter opened the door, his mouth went dry. The

beautiful, clumsy customer from the week before stood there looking like she would rather punch him out than allow him into her home.

Chapter 15

*O*h, this can't be happening. This guy? I guess I shouldn't be surprised that the man who is rude to customers also doesn't care about getting side jobs done in a timely manner. Lord, please let whatever plumbing problem there is be fixed as quickly as possible.

She looked past him and was disappointed that Joe was not there; the last thing she wanted was to have to make small talk with him. She turned on her heel as she motioned toward the damaged area. Hearing her mother's voice in her head chastising her for being so rude to a stranger who was there to help her made her want to do it more. She reminded herself that she was an adult who didn't have to rebel against her mother and that she also placed a high priority on manners, and forced as civil a tone as she could manage.

"You must be Mitch; thank you for coming. Has Joe told you what happened here?"

"Yes, and I'm sure it will be a pretty easy fix. I'm sorry I wasn't able to get here sooner; I'll try to make it up to you by getting it done as fast as I can now that I'm here." He looked at her sheepishly. "Sorry about my tone at the hardware store the other day."

She tried to ignore the flutters in her stomach when he half-smiled at her and she reminded herself not to be charmed. There was a kindness in his eyes that she hadn't seen a few days earlier when he was glowering at her. Her days of being manipulated and excusing bad behavior were over, though, and after the way he had acted at the hardware store the apologetic look and tone only served to fuel her irritation.

"It's fine. You probably don't usually have customers destroy your store on their first visit. Do you think you can fix this?"

He snickered as if she had just asked him if he knew how to turn on a faucet. "Yeah."

His arrogance made her want to tell him to leave; his laugh made her feel like another tree had just hit. Both made her want to get away from him.

Thankfully, Joe walked in and broke the tension she was feeling. She excused herself and went into the bedroom to catch her breath. *No, no, no. This is no time to be attracted to a jerk with nice eyes and a great smile. You don't do that anymore, remember?*

She stood by the door and listened to the two men talk about what needed to be done, and was relieved when she heard Mitch say that he had the supplies they would need in his truck and that they could probably get it fixed in a few hours. She was also disappointed that he would be done and out of there so quickly, and chastised herself again. It wasn't until she exhaled when she heard Mitch walk out to his truck for supplies that she realized she had been holding her breath.

Chapter 16

Mitch forced himself to calm his breathing as he walked to the truck. The fiery brunette had plenty of attitude and sure knew how to get a man's goat. *Keep your distance from that one. Get the job done fast and get out.*

He was usually glad that he always kept a variety of supplies in his truck for occasions like this; it saved him a lot of time running back and forth when he was doing jobs. Today he wished he had reason to go back to the store, but figured it would be just as helpful to get the job done in record time and get out. Since Joe was there too, it would be a fast fix. Joe would also be a good buffer between him and the angry renter.

He couldn't decide which picture was more dangerous to have in his mind: the one of her eyes full of fire and fury or the twinkle he first saw at the hardware store. Either way she was trouble, and he planned to keep his distance.

As he was laying out tools and supplies on the step to take up to the apartment, his phone rang and he saw that it was Cynthia. Phone calls were generally reserved for emergencies, so he knew it was no social call.

"Hi, sis."

"I need you here now." There was panic in her whispered tone and he knew there was no time to waste. Something was going on with Zack and he needed to get there as quickly as possible.

"I'm on my way." He hopped into the truck and headed to her house, leaving the pipes and tools he'd piled on the steps and forgetting about the job he had been in the middle of doing.

He called Cynthia's friend and police deputy Wyatt Henry on the way to give him a heads-up that they may need his help. Mitch and Cynthia had sat down with him several weeks before to come up with a plan in case the day came when Zack's issues would come to a head and intervention would be necessary. Wyatt had assured them that whether or not he was working, he would be there. He had the experience and the temperament to handle the situation, and Zack knew and trusted him. His years as an MP in the Marines and as a deputy in Hideaway had given him all the experience he needed to be on the front lines with them. Fortunately, it just so happened that he was on duty.

When Mitch got off the phone with him and remembered the job he'd left behind, he called Joe, too.

"I'm sorry I had to take off. Zack is having a bad enough episode that Cynthia asked me to come right over. Tell the renter I'll get back there as soon as possible and that I'm sorry."

"I assumed as much when I heard you leave. Don't worry about this; I'll explain and do what I can to start things here. I'll be praying, and let me know if you need anything."

"At this point, just prayers."

He wished he knew how to pray better himself, but was glad for friends who knew more about it than him. If he ever needed to talk to God, this was the time.

He looked up toward the sky and decided to try it for himself the way he'd seen Joe, Clay, and Wyatt do it. "God, I don't know if I'm doing this right, but please help us here. Please help Zack and show us what to do for him." He had always felt like God was there for him, and even felt protected on the battlefield; he didn't know why he still felt awkward praying or talking or whatever it was he was doing. Even though he wasn't sure if he was doing it right, it felt good to lean on Him a bit and gave him some peace.

Chapter 17

Bella heard the tires kicking up gravel in the driveway as Mitch suddenly left. *Of all the nerve! So much for his apology for being late. Honestly, how does this man get hired if this is the care he takes with jobs?*

It took a few breaths to settle down her anger and bring her blood back down below the boiling point. She reminded herself that Joe was not responsible for Mitch's behavior before going back into the living room.

"Did your friend leave?"

"Yes, and he asked me to apologize for him. He had an emergency come up, but he said he'll get back here as soon as he can."

"I hate to sound insensitive, but do you have any idea how long this 'emergency' might take?"

He looked at her apologetically. "No way to tell. The good news is that he was able to look at it and see what needs to be done and left tools and supplies out before he got called away. I can get started without him and do a good portion of the work myself. It will just take longer. I'm really sorry."

"It's not your fault. It's hard to get reliable help these days." Sounding like her mother sent a pang of guilt through her. She shot up a quick prayer in case what took Mitch away really was an emergency, even though she doubted it.

Just then, her phone rang and she saw that it *was* her mother. *Just what I need. I guess that's what I get for acting like her.* She silenced the ringer and grabbed her purse.

"Do you need me for anything, Joe?"

"No, I'll do what I can here and I'll let you know when I hear back from Mitch. I apologize again."

"It's okay. I apologize for sounding as frustrated as I am; I know it's not your fault. I'm just going to run to the store. Can you lock up if you leave before I get back?"

"Sure."

It took all of her willpower not to slam the door on her way out, but she succeeded in closing it calmly. She didn't want to get a reputation so soon in her residency.

She needed to drive. She needed the wind in her hair and loud music in her ears before she called her mother back. Not knowing where else to go, she headed in to Lakes End to sit by the beach and look at Sapphire Lake, hoping that the calming sight would help her to feel ready to talk to her mother.

As she waited for her to pick up, she felt the knot start in her stomach. *So much for the calming sight making this easier.*

"Isabella." She had the warmth of a marble statue.

"Hello, Mother. I saw that you called."

"I've just learned that you moved out of your house. Where are you?" *Great. She's been talking to Harrison. She always liked him better than me, anyway. I shouldn't be surprised that he's getting her in the divorce.*

"I'm in Michigan, and of course I moved out of the house. That's what people do when they get divorces." She felt a little giggle rise up when she said the D word to her mother. She felt like a rebellious child who had just sworn in front of her parents.

"The proceedings aren't final, Isabella. There's still time to come to your senses and go home. No one knows what you've done and I think Harrison will still take you back."

"What *I've* done? How is divorcing an adulterer somehow worse than *being* an adulterer, Mother?"

"Well, I see you're still holding on to fairy tales. Will you please send me your address so I know where you are?"

"Yes. Is there anything else?"

"No, I just wanted to check in on you." *More like check up on me, but whatever.*

"I'll talk to you soon, Mother. I need to go."

Between rude workmen and rude mothers, Bella had had it. She turned her phone off and took a cold walk through town.

Chapter 18

When Mitch arrived at Cynthia's house, she looked even more panicked than she had sounded on the phone.

"Where is he?"

"He's locked himself in his room. I've been trying to get him to come out and up until fifteen minutes ago, he was talking. Now he's silent and–" She couldn't continue as the tears spilled down her cheeks. Mitch gave her shoulder a quick squeeze as he walked toward Zack's door. He was thankful that they had swept the place for firearms the day before and found none.

"Hey, buddy, it's me. Can I come in?" No answer, but he could hear Zack's heavy breathing. "Listen, if you need time alone, I get it. We just need to know that you're okay. Can you just let me know you're alright?"

He looked at Cynthia. She was frozen in place and he knew what she was thinking. He hated to take any action that might scare Zack, but he also knew the statistics on suicide for veterans, especially those with Post-Traumatic Stress, and wasn't taking any chances.

"Buddy, I need to open your door. Your mom needs to see that you're okay. Will you unlock the door? I don't want to have to break it down, but you've got us scared here."

When Zack didn't respond, Mitch turned to his sister and whispered, "Call Wyatt. Tell him no sirens."

Mitch continued talking through the door while he waited for Wyatt to get there. He would know what to do and hopefully everything could end peacefully. He sent a quick text to Clay and Joe.

"Zack locked himself in his room. Wyatt is on the way. Time for more serious action. Please pray."

Wyatt entered the house quietly and had another deputy with him, along with two EMT's. They had worked out the details of how to handle this situation if it ever came to pass months ago, with Zack being an active participant in the discussion. They were as prepared as they could be. Wyatt gestured to Cynthia to go outside before he gave Mitch the nod to proceed and took his place behind him.

Mitch took a deep breath. "Zack, Wyatt is here with me, and I'm going to need to bust this door down now, okay? You stay back from it."

He hit the door with his shoulder and was relieved that the lock gave way on the first try. Zack just stared blankly at him as he lay in the fetal position on his bed. Mitch slowly approached him and Wyatt followed. He remained frozen as they sat on either side of him.

"You're going to be okay, Buddy. Remember how we planned for this. We're going to get you someplace safe and get you the help you need."

Zack just nodded.

Wyatt reminded him in a calm voice that they were going to restrain him for his safety and motioned to the other deputy and the EMT's to move in. Zack finally found his voice as he looked at Mitch with blank eyes.

"Don't let my mom see me."

"Okay. She's outside. Can I call her and let her know you're okay?"

Zack nodded. The look in his eyes broke Mitch's heart. He looked like a combination of a young child full of fear and a zombie. Mitch put his hand on his shoulder and dialed with the other as Wyatt and the deputy carefully put the restraints on him.

"Zack is okay and he's letting us get him the help he needs. He can't talk to you right now and doesn't want you to see him like this. Can you go somewhere while we get him set?"

"Okay, I'll go over to Evelyn's. Tell him I love him and update me as soon as you can."

"Will do."

Zack let the EMT's and deputies help him onto the stretcher and strap him down, and stared at Mitch while they gave him a sedative.

"We're coming with you, Zack. Wyatt will be in the ambulance and I'll be right behind you in my truck. You're not going to be alone." Mitch breathed a sigh of relief and fought tears as Zack fell asleep. He sent the first of many update texts to Cynthia, then sent up the first of many more prayers.

Lord, please get the VA to listen and do something now.

∞∞∞

Mitch listened quietly as Zack calmly answered the nurse's questions. The hospital was admitting him for his safety and Zack seemed okay with it, maybe even relieved. Before the nurse left the room, she gestured to the restraints still on his arms and legs.

"I'm sorry that these have to stay in place while you're in the ER. They'll take them off as soon as you get to your unit. Are you comfortable?"

"Yes, thank you."

Mitch walked closer to the bed when she left the room and put his hand on Zack's arm.

"You okay, Buddy?"

Zack's face was expressionless. "I didn't mean to scare anybody. I wasn't going to hurt myself."

"I know. Remember what we agreed to, though. Our main focus is keeping you safe, and if they can help you here, this is the best place for you. We don't want you to get to the point where you do try to hurt yourself. And they're going to work with the VA and the Veteran's Ranch to see if they can get you moved up the waiting list at one of them."

"Thanks for convincing my mom not to come here. I don't want her to see me like this."

"I know; I don't either. I've been texting her and telling her that they're taking care of you and that you're okay. She told me to kiss you for her, but I told her not to be gross."

He was relieved when Zack gave a weak laugh. "Don't you dare kiss me."

Mitch reached over and bumped fists with him, then held his hand. "We love you, Buddy, and we're here for you. We're done messing around here and we're going to do everything in our power to get you the help you need."

"Thanks . . . for everything."

The orderlies came in just then to move him to the psychiatric unit. As they wheeled him out of the room, Mitch picked up the bag that held Zack's personal items. Something about seeing his shoelaces in there along with his wallet, phone, and keys made the reality of how bad off Zack was hit Mitch square in the jaw and he stopped fighting the tears that he'd been holding back since they got there.

As he was driving home, he called Cynthia to give her an update and reassure her that Zack was doing as well as could be expected and to set up a time for them to go visit him in the morning. His next call was to Joe to ask if he or Emily could cover any time in the store in the morning while he and Cynthia went to the hospital.

He longed for his bed and was counting the minutes until he would get home when he remembered the angry renter and the work he was doing such a terrible job at completing. Sighing, he changed routes and headed to Nancy Pullman's place. When he tried to call Nancy to warn her he was coming back, he could only leave a voice mail. He hoped it wouldn't be too rude to stop by so late to work on the apartment, but it seemed to be the least rude option if the other one was putting off the job for another day.

Since the woman already seemed to hate him, he figured he had nothing to lose. He saw light coming from the apartment window as he pulled into the drive, so he decided to take a chance.

Her surprise quickly turned to irritation when she saw him standing there at her door. He hoped the peace offering he'd brought in the form of a variety of wall hooks would give him some points.

"Sorry for stopping by so late. I couldn't get in touch with Nancy and didn't have a number for you. Would you like me to work on it now or would you rather have me come back tomorrow evening?"

She sighed and glared at him. "Come in."

He shivered as he walked in the door. "It's freezing in here."

"Joe said not to turn the electricity back on until you gave the okay, so it's *been* freezing in here."

That explained her frosty tone as well as the sweatshirt-robe-blanket combo she was wearing and the room full of candles.

"Sorry again. I had an emergency I needed to take care of earlier, or I would have been done with this by now. I'll make sure it's safe and get you some heat, if nothing else, tonight."

He gave what he hoped she would see was an apologetic look as he held out the bag in his hand. "Wall hooks, on the house."

Her eyes widened and face softened a bit as she took the bag. "Thank you."

He was relieved that she turned quickly and he hoped she didn't see the heat rise in his face when their hands touched as she took the bag. *Focus, man. This chick is trouble.*

He made his way over to the exposed pipes and carefully examined the area that Joe had worked on earlier. He wished Joe was there now, because he needed an extra set of hands to finish it and the last thing he wanted was to be in close proximity to her. Realizing he had no choice if he wanted to make it stable and safe for her to have some heat for the night, he bit the bullet and asked for help.

"Miss?"

"It's Bella."

"Bella. Could you help me out for a minute here? I need someone to hold the pipe while I attach this to stabilize it."

She sighed and looked as if she needed to decide if it was worth it, then put her blanket down and approached him. "Tell me what to do."

Chapter 19

B ella willed her hands to steady and reminded herself to breathe as she held the pipes the way he showed her. Keeping her eyes fixed on the pipe and trying to avoid noticing his arms and rough hands or the faint scent of his aftershave were not an easy task. She hoped the candlelight kept it dark enough that he couldn't see her blush as their arms interlocked, and looked away just in case.

It was bad enough that she'd had to turn away when they accidentally touched as he gave her the bag of wall hooks; having ongoing contact like this was almost too much for her. She reminded herself that irresponsible, arrogant jerks weren't her type and focused on her job.

"Can you move your hand a little bit that way? This is rusted on and isn't budging."

When he spoke, she made the mistake of looking up at him. When their eyes met, she felt like she turned into putty. Just then, he jerked his hand back and grunted. She looked over to see that he had lost his grip and cut himself.

"Oh no!" As she ran to grab a towel, he held his hand up and tried to stop the blood from dripping onto the floor. She didn't think as she carefully wrapped it and held it tightly to stop the bleeding. She looked up at him to find his face dangerously close to hers and quickly looked down. He took over holding the towel as she stepped back away from him.

"You didn't cut it on the rusty part, did you?"

"No, I don't think so."

She picked up her phone and turned on the flashlight to get a better look. "Do you think it needs stitches?"

He snickered. "It's just a scratch. I'll be fine." It seemed to be bleeding pretty badly, and she hoped he wasn't just being macho. When she glanced into his eyes again, she noticed how tired he looked and realized how long he had been there.

"We don't have to finish this tonight. You probably need to get home."

"I promised I would get you some heat for the night, and I keep to my word." He chuckled, "Well, usually. You haven't seen much evidence of that."

She felt herself soften and couldn't help but laugh with him. "No, not really. But I don't want you hurting yourself, and you're obviously exhausted."

He sighed. "It's been a long week. If you don't mind giving me a few more minutes, I'll get things safe for you to turn the electricity back on and then I'll get out of your hair. Fixing it is going to take longer than I thought, but stabilizing it and getting it safe for the night should be quick."

"Okay. Let me at least find you a bandage for that cut, though."

They went back to their positions by the pipes and got back to work once the cut on his hand was sufficiently covered. He was able to quickly stabilize the pipes and took a last look with the flashlight.

"Okay, it's all set. I'll go turn the electricity back on."

As he went down into the garage to turn the electricity on, she let out a sigh of relief. *Wow. That was way too much.*

Bella had never been around someone so . . . *manly.* He was nothing like the corporate types who didn't even know what a wrench was, let alone how to use one. She told herself she was just intrigued by someone different from what she was used to. She was lost in thought as she compared his rough, strong hands to Harrison's smooth, manicured ones and jumped when he reappeared in the doorway.

"I can come back early in the morning if it's okay with you."

"Now that I have electricity, I'll have the coffee pot on by 6:30." She felt the heat on her cheeks again as he looked at her and nodded, and was glad she hadn't turned any of the lights back on yet.

The next morning, she woke up early and found herself looking at the clock frequently as she waited for Mitch to return. "It's just water, that's all. You just want him here to fix the pipes so you can take a shower here again."

It was purely coincidental that she had put on her favorite new sweater, and she was just being efficient by putting on her makeup for the day while the coffee brewed.

He showed up at exactly 6:30 am with a bag of donuts that smelled like nothing she'd ever experienced. "If you haven't tasted the nutty crescent donuts from the bakery yet, you haven't really lived."

He stifled a yawn as she took the bag from him, careful to avoid any more accidental contact.

"Thank you for bringing breakfast. Coffee is coming right up."

"Maybe if I have some coffee, I won't make any more mistakes that get my hands cut up."

"How is it doing today?"

"It's deeper than I thought last night, so I may have someone look at it when I go to the hospital in a couple of hours." He must have read the concern on her face, because he added, "I'm going to visit someone."

She took a bite of the donut and thought she'd died and gone to heaven. "Oh my goodness, this is the best donut I've ever tasted."

"Told you." He had the best smile she'd ever seen, but she told herself it was just the donut talking.

Chapter 20

Between the throbbing in his hand and the enticing assistant so close, Mitch had a hard time focusing on his task. He was glad he'd texted Joe and asked him to meet him there. His arrival would help with both problems.

Mitch's hand was practically useless, but he ignored the pain and tried working on the pipe. The wrench dug into the cut and he stifled a word his mother taught him not to say.

"I'm sorry. Between these rusted pipes and this cut, I'm not sure I'm going to be as useful or as fast as I would like to be. You're right that it probably needs some stitches."

"If you need to go get it taken care of, it's fine. You don't need to make it worse."

"It's okay. My sister and I are going to the hospital in a few hours and I'll take care of it then. Joe should be here soon and I can direct him."

The idea that he would need to do much directing almost made him laugh. They had each taught the other a lot about their respective areas of expertise, and Joe was a fast learner. He probably could have checked out the plumbing himself, but trusted Mitch's judgment more than his own. He was also always good about throwing work Mitch's way during the slow months at the hardware store, so he didn't hesitate to call him for jobs.

"Is that what your emergency was yesterday?" She barely had

the question out when she waved her hands as if she was trying to erase it. "Sorry, I take that back. It's none of my business. Why don't you sit down and finish your coffee and donut while they're both still warm?"

"Sure." He sat on the couch and looked at the overstuffed chair she had sat in. It was at an odd angle to the couch and the rest of the room.

She saw the curious look on his face and laughed. "Here. You're the guest and you're injured. Sit here and see why I moved it there." She stepped away from the chair and motioned for him to move over to it.

When he sat down, she pointed toward the window. With the chair at that angle, he could see a bit of Sapphire Lake in all its splendor. He smiled at the beautiful shades of blue. "Ahh, now I see the purpose for the unique decorating."

"It took me a while to get that at just the right angle, but now I start every day there. It's hard to leave that spot when my coffee cup is empty and I have to get up."

"I can see why." He looked from the lake to her face and her eyes looked like they'd been painted with the same sapphire brush. He scrambled for an excuse to look away before it was too late.

"My hand works enough to install wall hooks. Can I put those up for you while I'm here? It's the least I can do after chasing you out of the store before you could get them the other day." He gave her a sheepish smile and hoped she'd forgiven him for being so rude that day.

She smiled and looked at him apologetically. "I'm sorry for ruining your store, *and* for giving you attitude about leaving yesterday. I didn't realize you had a real emergency. I just figured after you hadn't shown up . . ."

"That I was an irresponsible loser who didn't do what he said he would do?"

She chuckled. "Something like that. I hope everything turns out okay for whoever is in the hospital."

"I think it will. He'll be okay." He stood up. He wasn't about to get into Zack's personal business with someone he didn't know and who may still think he was an irresponsible loser.

"Where do you want those wall hooks?"

As she showed him where she wanted the hooks in the tiny area that passed for a kitchenette, he reminded himself that he was just there for a job, not for enjoying the company of an attractive woman. Joe saved the day by knocking on the door just as their eyes locked again.

"I got here as early as I could, but had to wait for Emily to come to my house to be there when Lily woke up. It's going to be nice on mornings like this when we all live under one roof."

"Those pipes are all ready for you." Mitch pointed him in the direction of the pipes he'd been struggling with and finished up with the wall hooks. At least he could finish one thing he started.

When he returned to Joe's side and they started back on the pipes, he felt his hand starting to get wet and looked down to see that it was bleeding again. Bella noticed it, too, and went to get the bandages.

As he sat at the small desk that doubled as the only table in the apartment, she carefully unwrapped the gauze. He tried to focus on anything but her tender touch and the tiny shots of electricity he felt with every brush of her hand against his. He was thankful that she kept her eyes on his hand instead of meeting his gaze.

Joe stepped over to look at it, too. "That's ugly, man. Maybe you and Cynthia should head to the hospital now and get that taken care of."

Bella nodded in agreement. "I appreciate you trying to get this done, but I don't need water that badly. I'll just take showers at Nancy's until this is done here. Go get your stitches and let me know when you're coming back."

Mitch and Joe shared a look. Mitch drew in a slow breath before carefully breaking the bad news. "I'm sorry to tell you this, Bella, but my getting stitches isn't the only thing that's going to make this job take time." She frowned as he continued. "We need to re-place more pipes than the ones that were damaged by the storm; they're in bad shape."

He braced himself for her wrath to return, but she just sighed and said, "Okay. I kind of figured that might happen after watch-ing you two. Take whatever time you need." He was relieved that he hadn't ticked her off again and that she was understanding.

Joe gave her a reassuring look. "I'll do everything else that I can before I go, and I'll see if my fiancée can come help me."

"Your fiancée can do repairs?"

Joe beamed. "Emily can do just about anything."

Mitch laughed. "I'm going to miss that puppy dog look when you get married, Joe. It's cute."

Joe laughed along with him. "I'm down to counting days until my wedding, so you're going to have to just deal with my happi-ness."

After years of seeing his friend's sorrow, he was more than glad to deal with his happiness. He envied him; he couldn't imagine feeling happy and in love like that. The closest he'd ever come to that ended in heartbreak and humiliation, and he still wasn't ready to take that chance again.

Chapter 21

Bella took in the look on Joe's face. *Oh, to be loved like that.*

She wasn't sure if she had ever been around anyone who looked so smitten. No, that wasn't true. Dani's husband looked like that when he watched her walk down the aisle at their wedding. Seeing it on his face had made Bella believe love was possible . . . at least for some people.

She quickly wrapped Mitch's hand in fresh gauze and taped it tightly to limit the bleeding before sending him on his way to the hospital. She ignored her disappointment that he was leaving and focused on what Joe was saying. He was texting his fiancée while they talked to try to arrange a way to get her there quickly.

∞∞∞

Emily arrived soon after Mitch left, and Bella was impressed with both her skill and the couple's ability to work together. The absence of harsh words and passive-aggressive comments was re-freshing, even if it made Bella feel like she was observing alien life forms.

Just as Nancy said she would, she felt an immediate connection with Emily. She had only moved to Hideaway the previous fall, so she was still fairly new in town, but it seemed she had acclimated easily. The two women got a chance to get to know each other a bit when Joe went to open Mitch's hardware store.

"This is a great area and I would be happy to show you around if you'd like. The people are some of the nicest I've ever known."

"What brought you here?"

Emily looked thoughtful. "I needed a new life. I had just got-ten out of a bad marriage to a bad guy and needed a new start. I wanted something completely different from metro Detroit, where I grew up, and LA, where I had been living for several years. My family thought I was crazy, but I just drove and asked God to show me where to stop. Less than 24 hours after arriving here, I knew this was the place. There was just something special here." She grinned as if lost in the memory. "Eventually I met Joe, and the rest is history."

Bella smiled. "You two seem well-suited for each other. I was surprised at how well you worked together."

Emily laughed as she looked over at the damaged wall. "Actu-ally, we got to know each other over a plumbing problem and renovation at the B and B where I live. I got cheap rent for helping with cleaning and getting some unused rooms ready for guests, and when there was a leak and the job turned from cleaning and minor sprucing up to repairing and renovating, Joe and Mitch helped out. I had experience working with renovation, so Joe and I spent hours working together to repair the damage; somewhere in the middle of sanding and refinishing floors, we fell in love. What brought you here?"

Bella chuckled at the similarities. "Well, I see why Nancy wanted us to meet. I needed a fresh start after getting out of a bad marriage, too. My husband wasn't a bad guy per se, but he and I had different ideas about marriage. My idea was that once you get married, you stop dating other people, for example." She rolled her eyes and Emily grimaced and nodded as if she knew what that was like. "When I left him, my family was shocked and horrified. To them, divorcing a spouse is apparently worse than cheating on one, so they're barely speaking to me. When I started my new life, I had no hometown to return to, so I came to the one place I remembered from a childhood vacation, even though I had to Google it to find out where it was. I decided I would give it six months, and if I liked it, I would stay." Emily was easy to talk to and it felt good to be open and honest about what brought her here.

"Well, I can tell you this is the best place in the world for a new start. I had a lot of healing to do when I first arrived, and it took no time at all. This place has magical healing powers."

"I can see that. And big trees." As they looked at the damaged wall and shared a laugh, it felt like they were already friends.

By the time Emily had to leave, they had exchanged numbers and Bella had accepted her invitation to join them at church on Sunday. Bella once again thanked God for leading her back to Summit County; this was a place she could call home.

Chapter 22

Mitch was glad to walk into the hardware store after getting his hand stitched up and visiting with Zack. The store had always felt like an extension of home to him, and it made him feel like things were settling down when he walked in and smelled the coffee Joe had just made.

"You've got perfect timing with the coffee. I brought lunch."

"Thanks, I'm starving. How's Zack?"

"He's actually doing well. Even though he hates taking medications, he was very happy to get a full night of sleep last night. The hospital is working with the Veteran's Ranch, too, and they think he can go there in a few days."

"Wow, that's great news. If the place is anything like what you've heard, it will be a good thing for him. If you need me to cover the store while you take him down there, just say the word."

"I appreciate that. I feel bad that it's one more thing to take us away from finishing Bella's place; I'd like to get it done as soon as possible."

Joe looked at his bandaged hand. "It doesn't look like you'll be doing much with that hand for a while. Did you get stitches?"

"Yep. They said I just missed the tendon." *That's what you get for getting lost in the eyes of a troublesome woman.*

"Emily went over and helped earlier, so the project is moving along. We'll get it taken care of. I just wish the timing was different and it wasn't right before we leave."

"Well, you could just put off the honeymoon until the project is done." Mitch laughed as he prepared to dodge a flying object.

Joe threw a napkin at him. "Not a chance."

Just as they were finishing their lunch, Bella walked in the door. He tried not to notice his pulse quicken when he looked at her.

"Uh-oh, that's a lot of bandage. How many stitches?"

"Fifteen. Like I said, just a scratch."

She shook her head and rolled her eyes. "Macho men."

"What can I do for you? I'd be happy to go get whatever you need so I don't have another crashed display on my hands."

Joe looked at him and stifled a laugh as he must have realized that Bella was the beautiful but clumsy customer Mitch had told him about earlier in the week.

"Actually, I'm here to apply for a job."

Mitch laughed and almost choked on his coffee. "A *what*?"

She held his gaze. "A job. I need a temporary job and from what I hear, you need a temporary employee."

Joe turned to him so that Bella couldn't see the amused look on his face. "That sounds like a perfect solution to your problem, Mitch. Zack will be gone for a while, and I'm sure Bella will be a fine replacement."

"You're kidding, right? You tried to destroy my store when you were just shopping. I'm afraid of what would happen if I gave you full reign."

"I had a klutzy *moment*, but I promise I won't destroy your store. Give me a probationary week and see."

She looked at his heavily wrapped hand and added, "No pun intended, but you need an extra set of hands around here."

"You're serious."

"I'm as serious as a big tree in a tiny apartment. When can I start?"

Wow, she's a persistent one. Okay, I can tolerate her for a while; I just need to keep my distance and not look at her.

"How about now? There are some boxes of seed packets on the back shelf that arrived yesterday. Can you put them on the display without breaking anything?"

"Watch me."

Oh, I won't be watching you if I can help it.

As she went to the back, Joe grinned at him. "Good luck with that." He laughed as he walked out the door.

Bella picked up on things quickly, to Mitch's surprise. When they had first met, she had a way about her that suggested that she was more boarding school than shop class, but she was showing that she was a hard worker and might be able to fit in just about anywhere.

She was eyeing the store as if she was studying it while she swept the floor. "Mitch, I don't want to tell you how to run your business, but do you ever put seasonal items over here so customers will see them as soon as they walk in?"

"No, I put things where they go." *What have I gotten myself into?*

"Well, I won't bore you with numbers or research studies, but if you put some of that gardening and spring cleaning stuff up here in the front, you'll sell a whole lot more of it than if you keep it 'where it goes'." He chuckled at her overly dramatic use of air quotes. "You'll be doing your customers a favor by reminding them that they need things they didn't come in here for and you'll save them a trip."

The last thing he needed was someone coming in and telling him how to run his business, but what she said made sense and he kicked himself for not thinking of it.

"Okay, you can put things up there for now. They'll get the same probationary period that you're getting."

"Perfect. We'll both show you our worth." She grinned as she went to fetch the displays.

Chapter 23

Bella was glad Emily had invited her to go to church, especially when she found out that they went to the small white church with the tall steeple that she had noticed the first time she came down the hill into town. She had told herself she would go there after she got settled in, and the invitation gave her reason to go sooner rather than later. *Thank You, Lord, for working things together as You always do.*

She wasn't sure why she was nervous; it hadn't been *that* long since she'd been. She had never been to a church that was so small or so charming, and she hoped the people inside were as genuine as Emily and Joe. Her experience with churches had run the gamut from impressive buildings with people inside trying to be equally impressive to high school gymnasiums with people inside who were there serving God and each other. She hoped this church was more like the latter, and vowed to find another one soon if it wasn't.

Emily met her inside the entrance, where she introduced her to her landlady, Evelyn Glover. She was as warm as Emily and quickly invited Bella to join them all for lunch at her home after the service.

"I've been mostly eating out of boxes since the tree made its way into my apartment, so I would love to. I would also love to see the work that Emily and Joe did there."

"Making sure our work is quality before you let us do more at your place?" Joe had slipped in behind Bella and teased her as he made his way over to kiss Emily on the cheek. His daughter leaned out of his arms to grasp Emily as soon as she saw her, and Emily hugged her as if she hadn't seen her in a week. When Emily had talked about her the day before, it was obvious that she adored the little girl; it warmed Bella's heart to see that the feeling was mutual.

"I've heard enough about the quality of your work since I've been in town to trust that you'll do a wonderful job. The way Emily described what you did made me want to see what it looks like in person. And this must be Lily."

Joe beamed with pride as he looked at the little girl. "Yes, this is the one and only. I'll let you ladies go upstairs and get settled and meet you up there in a minute."

Bella followed Emily, Lily, and Evelyn up the stairs to the sanctuary and fell more in love with the old church with each step. The building had such history and warmth to it that she hoped even more that it would be a good fit for her.

She sat in the middle of the row next to Emily while Evelyn joined a friend on the other side of the aisle. As she watched people greet each other and catch up on their lives before the service started, she felt like she had just walked into a movie that was set in a small town. It was a striking contrast to any other place she'd lived.

"Does everyone here know everyone else?"

Emily chuckled. "Yes, but don't worry; you'll know them all soon, too. Everyone was so welcoming to me when I moved here and now I forget sometimes that I haven't even lived here for a year yet. They treat me like they've known me forever, too."

While Emily retrieved some children's Bible stories from her bag to entertain Lily, Bella looked around. She was unprepared for the emotion she felt sitting there watching everyone get settled in their seats and chat with their friends.

The longest she had lived anywhere was six years, and that was in Dallas where her main role was being Harrison's wife. She never felt at home there, and didn't know what it was like to feel truly welcomed. With all the moving around that her family did, she had learned not to get too attached to a place or to the people who lived in it. It was a strange feeling being in a place where she *wanted* to be a part of things and be known.

"When my family moved to new towns, my parents always immediately joined the country club and whichever church most of its members went to. They were never concerned with what was being spoken from the pulpit, if they even heard a word. They just sat quietly staring ahead and made sure my sister and I did the same. They wouldn't have known what to do with themselves in a place like this."

"The town or the church?"

Bella laughed. "Both, although they did seem to like the town when we vacationed here. I think they were so used to the big city and country club lifestyle that they never questioned it. I always hated it and they hated that about me. I never fit in any of those places." She felt tears stinging her eyes as she looked around. "I could stay here forever."

Emily leaned over and hugged her. "I hope you do."

Bella was surprised when she looked up and saw that Mitch was following behind Joe. Their eyes met and it was as if pieces that had been swirling in the air were falling into place for her; something felt very right about seeing him in the little church. When he smiled at her, she was glad she was already sitting down so it didn't matter that her knees suddenly went weak.

The pastor talked about the prodigal son, saying that everyone is a prodigal in one way or another, and that God is waiting to run toward them when they come home to Him. It felt like the message was written just for her and she felt the tears filling her eyes again. As she sat in the pew, she could almost feel His arms around her and smell the feast.

When Emily leaned over and whispered, "Your *heavenly* Father will never hate anything about you," and squeezed her hand, the tears spilled over. She felt like she had finally found home.

Chapter 24

Mitch was glad for the moments the last hymn gave him to absorb what Pastor Ray had said in his sermon. He had been nervous about finally accepting Joe's invitation to join them at church, but felt drawn to be there. After everything that had been going on with Zack, he finally felt as if he was leaning on God to do what he couldn't, and felt as if something was changing inside of him. Hearing about how God was always waiting for His children to return to Him and how He delighted in them touched a part of him that he didn't know needed it.

At the end of the hymn, Joe leaned over and said, "I think today was for you. I'm glad you're here."

"Me, too; and you only had to invite me for, what, six months?"

Joe had started inviting him as soon as he had started going again after his own two-and-a-half year absence from the pews following his first wife's death, and Mitch had put him off, just as he had put off Clay's invitation to the church that he attended on the other side of town. He wasn't sure why he had put it off, but was glad he'd finally taken the chance to walk through the door. It felt good and right to be there.

At the end of the service, Evelyn rushed over to hug him and invite him to lunch at her place. She had always been like a member of the family to him and he decided he could open the store a little bit late for one day in order to spend some time with her.

"You know I never turn down a meal at your house. I haven't been there in weeks, and I've been meaning to stop by."

"Don't you worry about it, dear. You've had your hands full lately, but Cynthia has kept you and Zachary on the top of my prayer list. I don't know why everything has been so much harder for him lately, but I have a feeling that he's on the mend now."

"I hope so, and appreciate the prayers. Can I stop and get anything to bring for lunch?"

"You know I always have more than enough food; Emily and I prepared and hoped for guests. I already invited Cynthia, too." After she hugged him again and went to speak to some of her friends, he turned to see Bella sitting quietly by herself in the pew looking at a stained-glass window as if lost in thought.

There was something different when their eyes met before the service; she looked like she had let down the defenses she seemed to surround herself with when they first spent time together. The way she had looked at him, as if she was actually glad to see him for a change, felt good. It almost felt good enough to quiet the voice in his head that told him to stay away from women who made him feel the way she did – almost.

He sat down next to her and hoped she wouldn't think he was intruding on her private moment. When she looked at him and he saw tears in her eyes, he had to fight the urge to put his arms around her and wipe them away. He always hated to see a woman cry, but this time it felt like his guts were twisting over it. He didn't know why; after all, he barely knew her and was not looking for romantic involvement.

She smiled at him and wiped her tears. "Don't worry, I'm not crazy or sad. I was just really touched by – well, everything here today."

"Me too. It's nice to see you here."

"You, too." Her smile was so genuine and soft. "This is your church, too?"

He looked down, suddenly feeling a little out of place and wishing he had a different answer. "No, this is my first time here for a service; actually, it's my first time in any church in a long time other than a couple of recent weddings."

"Mine too. It feels good, doesn't it?"

"It sure does." It felt good to be in church, and it also felt good to be sitting quietly with her.

When Joe approached the pew with Lily in tow, Mitch was disappointed that he was forced to break her gaze.

"You two ready to go? Emily and Evelyn went to get lunch set up."

Mitch and Bella looked at each other in surprise. "I guess we're having lunch together."

"I guess we are."

Chapter 25

Evelyn's home, the Shoreside Inn, was like something out of times gone by. Bella had seen the large Victorian house when she had driven down by Lake Michigan, and was mesmerized by it. She could see why Emily loved living there.

It was obvious that Evelyn loved maintaining it and took great care in keeping the décor to the original style. Bella felt like she could spend all day in the parlor or the small library, and when Emily showed her the work that she and Joe had done, she knew her perfect little apartment would once again be as wonderful as it was before the tree hit it. When Emily mentioned that Joe was an architect by training but had left it for the flexibility that came with doing renovation jobs and flipping houses when he became a single parent, Bella kicked herself for initially questioning his ability to restore her place.

Having lunch family-style at the large dining room table was a special treat. Bella struggled to think of the last time she had been at a table with so much easy conversation and so much warmth. These people were clearly all like family to each other, and she felt honored to be included. She couldn't help but sneak glances at Mitch; she'd never seen him so relaxed or smile so much. When she saw the funny faces he was making at Lily and his joy at the little girl's giggles, she couldn't look away.

His sister was much more talkative than he was, and she talked about what they had been going through with her son. He would soon be transferred to a ranch for veterans who were experiencing post-traumatic stress and had severe injuries, and Mitch and Cynthia were both obviously relieved that he was finally able to get to the head of the waiting list.

After lunch, Bella, Mitch, and Emily cleared the table while Joe put Lily in Evelyn's room for a nap and Cynthia and Evelyn went into the library. When Bella found herself alone with Mitch in the dining room, she took the opportunity to apologize again.

"Mitch, after hearing what you've been going through with your nephew, I feel even worse for how I acted before. I had no idea what was going on and I was too hard on you for not getting to the work on my place sooner. I'm sorry."

His soft smile melted her heart. "You couldn't have known. When I tore your head off at the store that first day, I was running on fumes after sleepless nights and that put me over the edge. That's no excuse for how I acted, though; I'm sorry."

"Apology accepted." She chuckled as she continued, "You know, now that the display is in the front of the store where it's not in the way – oops, I mean not *where it goes* – it's not getting knocked down."

"I'd say those probationary periods are going pretty well for both the display and the new temporary employee."

Their eyes locked and she felt drawn toward him as if a puppeteer was pulling her strings. Just as they started to move closer to each other, Emily walked back into the room. They both backed away, and Bella hoped Emily didn't realize what she'd just walked in on. She also hoped for another opportunity to pick back up where they'd just left off before chastising herself for feeling drawn to a man.

Chapter 26

Mitch was jarred back to reality when Emily walked into the room. He noticed the time and jumped.

"I completely forgot that I have to go open the store." He chided himself and forced himself to focus back on work. "You're still able to work in the morning, right? If I can get you up to speed quickly, then by the time I can use this hand again, you can watch the store alone while I finish up at your place."

"I'll be there."

Suddenly he was wishing he could fast-forward to Monday so that he could spend time with her, even if it was for training. He warned himself to be careful; he'd learned the hard way that women could be trouble, and the way she stirred parts inside of him that he had walled off years before made her more dangerous than most.

∞∞∞

That afternoon, Clay walked into the store with a big grin on his face.

"What's got you so happy?" *As if I don't know.* Clay had finally ended the 'just friends' game with Shelby, and had been walking on air since.

"I dropped Shelby off at home a while ago and found out I just missed you, so I thought I'd stop in to see how Zack is doing. Can't I just be happy to see a friend?"

Mitch laughed. "Yeah, that smile is not about seeing me; at least, it better not be. I take it things must still be going well with Shelby."

Clay's grin somehow got bigger. "It's been pretty amazing."

"Good for you." Mitch was happy for Clay. He was a good guy and had had his own bad experience with a woman in the past; he deserved someone genuine like Shelby. "I expected to see you two at Evelyn's when I was there for lunch today." Shelby was Evelyn's niece and lived at the Shoreside Inn, too.

"I got her to come to church with me and we ate lunch at my brother's." Clay pulled out two dollar bills and tossed them on the counter as he grabbed a bag of Cynthia's homemade snack mix. "What's going on with Zack? Any news on the Veteran's Ranch?"

"He should be able to go in a couple of days. He sounded good when I talked to him a while ago, and can't wait to get there. I think he's ready to dig in and do what he needs to do to get past this stuff."

"Anything I can do to help when you take him to the ranch? I can pull a shift or two here after work if you need me to. Since you haven't replaced the old cash register, I'm pretty sure I can work it as well as I did when I worked here in high school."

"Thanks, I'll let you know. Joe and Emily have offered, too, so if Cynthia lets me go, I'll set up a schedule. I think she's hoping to take him herself, but we'll see." He knew he should ask Clay the question that was burning in his head, but he felt like an idiot; touchy-feely conversations were not really his thing. He reminded himself that if there was anyone he could talk to about Bella, it was Clay. They had seen each other through the roughest times of their lives, and had had conversations that he had never had with anyone else. He took in a deep breath and was trying to spit it out when Clay beat him to it.

"So, who is this Bella person?"

Mitch couldn't stop his smile at the sound of her name and Clay let out a laugh. "I guess I'm not the only one smiling over a woman these days."

"She's just a friend, and I don't feel like swallowing a grenade again, so I'm not jumping into anything there."

"Are you sure about that? It looks like she's already hooked you. She seems nice, and Joe and Emily like her. What's the problem?"

"You know what the problem is. I've successfully avoided relationships since – well, for a long time. I can see her getting . . . dangerous."

Clay looked thoughtful. "You always said that you saw warning signs early on with Paula and ignored them; you ignored your gut. Do you see any of those warning signs with Bella?"

"No, none of the ones I saw in Paula. But I don't know her. She just blew into town a couple of weeks ago, and I don't know much about her."

"So find out. You ignored your gut before, but you learned that it was right. Why not follow it and see what happens with this one?"

"I'll think about it."

"You know I get not wanting to take the chance of getting burned again, but taking the risk with Shelby was one of the best decisions I've ever made. Take a chance, man. It might be worth it."

Maybe it's time.

Chapter 27

Bella finished her shift at the hardware store and headed home. She had successfully completed her training on the ins and outs of the store and was relieved that she had been able to avoid any klutz moments. She saw ideas everywhere she looked, but tried to hold back so that Mitch didn't feel like she was trying to take over. Since she had given 'helpful tips' on her first day, she tried to limit how many she offered on her second. He was a patient teacher, and she found herself wishing there was more training needed when they finished that afternoon. It appeared that she had passed his test, because he was letting her watch the store the next morning while he went to visit Zack, as long as she promised to call him or Joe with any questions or problems.

When she arrived at her apartment, Joe was replacing the last of the shingles on the roof and Emily was inside taking measurements of the damaged wall and ceiling. They were doing as much as they could without Mitch, and were coming to the end of what they could do until the plumbing was finished. Even though the water was still off, it felt like home again. As long as Bella sat facing the other direction, she could pretend that it was all finished.

Emily greeted her with a broad smile. "How was the hardware store?"

"I think I'm getting the hang of it. I never knew a hardware store could have so much unique stuff in it. I don't know if that's a small-town hardware store thing or if Mitch is a genius."

"From what I can see, it's a little bit of both. Joe said you got Mitch to try some new things. How did you manage that?"

Bella held the end of the measuring tape so that Emily could write while she measured. "I used my best salesmanship skills. I'm used to people resisting my ideas, then finding out that some of them are good. It's all part of the marketing territory."

"Have you had any luck finding a remote marketing job or any clients?"

"I've been talking to a couple of firms and potential clients, but no contracts have been signed yet. That's why I'm glad to have the hardware store; a little income is better than no income."

"Is the income the only thing you like about working at the hardware store?" Emily had a glint in her eye that suggested Bella's attempts to hide her attraction to Mitch weren't working.

"What do you mean?" She wasn't very good at playing dumb, but she also didn't want to admit anything either – most of all to herself.

Emily laughed. "I saw you two at Evelyn's after church yesterday. It was pretty obvious that you're enjoying each other's company, and he couldn't take his eyes off of you."

"Well, it needs to be just friendship and business at the moment; maybe for a long time. I'm not sure how long it will take to trust my people picker after doing such a bad job last time."

"Can I offer some advice? Let God do the picking this time. I don't know about you, but I know that when I chose to date and then marry my ex, I ignored everything my family and friends and my inner voice and God said about him. I overlooked his faults and thought that if I loved him enough, everything would be fine. By the time I got a glimpse of what kind of person he was, it was too late. We were married, and I was committed to making it work. It was only when I found out that he had broken not only our marriage vows but the law that I felt free to leave."

"That does sound pretty familiar, except that as far as I know, Harrison only broke marriage vows and the law of common decency. My family thought he was the perfect husband; they still think I should go back, even after what he did. I didn't realize that our definitions of what made a perfect husband were nowhere near the same until I left him. I thought I could love him enough and things would be okay, too, but like I told you, that didn't work out so well. Now I'm starting over and I'm on my own."

"Not completely." As Emily hugged Bella, she fought tears and thanked God for giving her a real friend in her new town.

"You're right; thank you for reminding me. I just don't know if I'm ready to try again or trust myself."

"I understand. I felt that way, too, and God reminded me that it was Him I was supposed to trust."

"Oh, so true. I definitely needed to hear that."

"And Mitch is a great guy. He was one of the first people I got to know here and he's one of the best."

Before Bella could respond, Joe walked in to announce that the roof was finished. When they left, Bella settled into her favorite chair and looked at the lake while she contemplated starting over and letting God be in charge of her relationships.

She pulled out her journal. It was time to stop beating herself up for choosing her family's approval over His leading when she decided to marry Harrison. It was also time to do what she had told herself for years that she had no right to do: ask God to help her clean up the mess she had created. *Okay, Lord, let's talk about this.*

That night she went to sleep with a smile on her face and peace in her heart. She knew that He forgave her and was with her, and the voice that had been accusing her and telling her for years that she got what she deserved, the one that she realized sounded suspiciously like her mother's, finally quieted.

Chapter 28

The time getting Bella up to speed in the store flew by, and Mitch allowed himself to enjoy being with a woman for the first time in years. There was something about her that was real and trustworthy, and it felt good to be around her. She took notes when needed about the way the store was run, and offered more suggestions that would help with product placement without getting pushy.

Since she picked up on things so quickly, he had left her in charge while he went to visit with Zack the last two mornings. Now that he was able to sleep uninterrupted at night, he was feeling much more productive, and it felt like his brain was firing on all cylinders again.

Zack and Cynthia were on their way to the Veteran's Ranch in Missouri, and Zack was looking forward to going through the 16-week program. Cynthia had insisted on driving him alone so that she could have time with Zack and Mitch could focus on taking care of things at home.

He walked into the store after sending off Zack and Cynthia and found Bella potting plants.

"What's this?"

"Don't get mad. I bought all the stuff so that if you didn't like my idea, I wouldn't get into trouble and I could take them to Nancy's. I just thought that if we had some pre-filled planters, it would give customers another reason to stop by the store during the spring and summer months. I wanted to show them to you instead of just telling you so that you could see how beautiful they can be."

He had to admit that it was a great idea – and that she was adorable when she was trying to talk herself out of getting into trouble with the boss.

"Don't tell Zack, but he's got competition for Employee of the Month. It's a great idea."

Just then, a woman came into the store and, seeing the planters, ordered four.

"Yup, you win. You get the parking space this month." He couldn't help but smile when he looked at her, and didn't want to stop.

She suddenly looked serious. "Mitch, thank you for letting me work here with you. It's helping me to feel settled here to have someplace to go every day while I figure out what I want to do with my life."

"I get the feeling you've got a lot of figuring to do."

She nodded as she looked off into space. "I do. I know I want to stay here, but beyond that, I don't know what else I want to do. At the end of the summer, Nancy's apartment will be closed up and I'll have to find a place to live. That's months away, so it's not a problem now, but between now and then, I need to figure out my other options, career-wise. I'm not used to having so much freedom of choice, and it's a little more complicated than I thought it would be."

He wasn't sure what she meant by that, but judging by the cloud that descended over her eyes, she was not always the free-spirited, independent woman that she appeared to be when she blew into town. He realized he didn't know that much about her other than that she was previously married, had worked in marketing, and that her family lived somewhere out west. All he knew was that he liked being around her; he also realized that he wanted to know everything about her. He wanted to swipe that cloud away and help her put down the roots she wanted to put down in Summit County.

"Well, if it helps at all, Zack is going to be gone for 16 weeks, and this job is all yours. I know it's not well-paying and it's not in your professional field, but it's yours if you want it."

"Are you saying my probationary period is over?"

"It may be the shortest probationary period in history, but you did what you said you would do; you proved your worth."

The smile she gave him warmed him, and he racked his brain to think of something he needed to do in the back of the store to give him some space. It was comfortable being with her, and that made him very *un*comfortable. He was torn between wanting to take her into his arms and wanting to run out the back of the store to get away from her and far from what he was starting to feel.

Chapter 29

Bella smoothed her skirt as she got ready for church and reminded herself that the most important part of going was the church part, not the 'I hope Mitch will be there' part. She was tired from fighting her attraction to him all week, and at the same time exhilarated from being near him. The guilt she felt for having such growing feelings for someone when she was still waiting for her divorce papers to show up signed was matched by the fear she felt of having growing feelings, period.

She didn't remember ever feeling such a powerful draw toward someone. She certainly never had flutters in her stomach when Harrison walked into a room or looked her way. It wasn't that she was never attracted to him; she was, and was happy with him when they were dating. They had dated on and off throughout high school and early in college and then got serious in their senior year. She had stars in her eyes back then, not necessarily about Harrison, but about marriage itself.

Her belief in happily-ever-after, and desire to have it as quickly as possible, led her to ignore all the evidence that was right in front of her that he was not someone she would find it with. She thought their marriage was her ticket out from under her parents and their stifling life; little did she know that she was going from stifling to suffocating when she walked down that aisle.

When she got to church, Mitch had just pulled into the space in front of her on the street. When he walked over and opened her car door, then offered his hand to help her from the car, she felt that flutter in her stomach again. It felt natural walking in with him and finding their way upstairs to the pew where they had sat the week before. By the time Joe and Emily came in, they were so engrossed in conversation that she hardly noticed until she heard Joe clear his throat.

Pastor Ray talked about God's generous love toward His children, and about the freedom He gives them to move on after hurts, heartaches, and mistakes. She felt as if the sermon had been written for her again as she thought about the way she had tried to pay penance for her past mistakes and failures as well as to control the future to avoid more. *Lord, thank You for releasing me from the past; I know my future is in Your hands and I know that there's nothing to fear. I give You my living situation, my career, and any potential relationship with Mitch or anyone else. While I'm at it, I give You the pain of never measuring up to my parents or to Harrison. Yours is the only opinion that matters to me.*

When they sang, "It is Well With My Soul" at the end of the service, she felt as if she could sing it from the rafters. For the first time in years, maybe forever, it was truly well with her soul.

Chapter 30

Mitch listened intently to the sermon. That morning he had been reading about the way Jesus cared for the hurting and for the people society had rejected, and the sermon seemed to go along nicely with it. He wondered if that sort of thing happened often; from what Clay had said, it seemed to. Clay had been thrilled when Mitch said he was finally going to church and reading the Bible he had given him, and he had answered all of the questions Mitch had after their run the day before.

Clay and Shelby were sitting across the aisle and at the end of the sermon, Clay made a point of nodding in his direction and giving him a knowing look. He knew God was teaching him and drawing him in, and whispered a prayer of thanks to Him for finally getting him through the church doors.

At the end of the service, he looked over at Bella and it was as if she was transformed. She had a look of contentment on her face that he hadn't seen before; she actually glowed. When she turned to him and smiled, he knew his days of fighting against his attraction to her were over. It would be a losing battle anyway, and was one he didn't want to fight anymore. If God was going to be there helping along this time, he was ready to take the risk; it might even be worth a little heartbreak to have some time with her.

He smiled at her sheepishly. "I hate to run, but I need to go get the store open. I know you volunteered to work today, but you deserve some time off. Plus, you look too pretty to be running around a hardware store."

"How am I going to maintain my Employee of the Month status if I don't work on weekends? Are you sure you're not just afraid of what suggestions I might make to improve things today? It's Sunday, so I'll keep my marketing mouth shut if you'd like." She had a sparkle in her eye as she teased him, and he had a feeling he was going to lose this battle, too. It was a battle he was glad to lose, because as much as he wanted to be a nice boss and a nice guy, he'd had to force himself to offer her the day off.

"You will not. That marketing mouth is making my customers happy and making me money. Would you like a ride to work?"

"Sure, I just need to get my sweatshirt and jeans out of my car."

He felt his own sense of contentment as they drove to the store and chatted about the sermon. He wasn't ready to get into the things from his past that he was feeling free from, and it seemed that she was feeling the same. Those conversations could wait, and he was intent on just enjoying being with her.

The day went fast, and before he knew it, it was time to lock up. It had been a fun day, with playful banter and laughter with Bella in between helping customers get supplies for spring cleaning and their gardens. He reminded the impatient gardeners of the dangers of planting in April, but knew it was falling on deaf ears, as usual.

When he drove her back to her car near the church, he found himself tongue-tied. He wanted to ask her out on a proper date, but lost both his words and his nerve when he looked into her eyes. She jumped out of his truck and into her car as soon as he stopped anyway, so it was just as well.

Chapter 31

B ella got out of Mitch's truck as quickly as she could. They had had a great day together, both at church and at the store. It seemed like there was a lightness and ease between them that hadn't been there before, and it was like a drug that she could become very addicted to very quickly.

When they were driving back to her car, Mitch had started shifting in his seat and fidgeting, as if he was nervous. Bella had initially gotten excited, thinking he might ask her out, but then had panicked. She couldn't very well go on a date while her divorce papers remained unsigned. It was bad enough that she hadn't told Mitch about her marital status; she was certainly not going to date while she remained someone else's wife. The irony was not lost on her that that was what her husband had been doing for years.

She prayed the whole way home for the right attitude and words to convince Harrison to sign the papers. As soon as she walked in the door, she dialed his cell number. *Please answer and let me get this phone call over with before I lose my courage.*

Harrison answered in his smooth, charming voice that told her that he was not alone and was looking to impress someone.

"Isabella, darling, I was just talking about you."

"With your attorney?"

He gave a hearty laugh. "Oh, how I miss your wit. I'm here at the club with the Klingensmiths and have been telling them about your creativity retreat. Are you ready to come home soon?"

When Satan hosts an ice cream social. "Harrison, you can tell anyone anything you want, but you need to sign the papers; you've had them for a month."

"I know; it's been too long. I miss you, too."

She stifled the urge to gag. "Sign the papers, Harrison." *Click.*

So much for having a good attitude and charming him.

She missed the days of flip phones. Tapping a screen was not nearly as satisfying as violently snapping a phone shut. What she wouldn't give for an old-fashioned landline that she could slam down in his ear.

"Lord, what is wrong with him? He's probably still talking as if I'm cooing on the other end of the phone."

She sent an email to her attorney to ask if there was a way to up the pressure on Harrison, then took a power walk to get away from her frustration.

Chapter 32

Mitch ended his call and heaved a sigh of relief. Zack sounded better than he had since – well, since Mitch didn't know when. He walked back up to the front of the store and Bella seemed to read the relief on his face.

"He's adjusting down there?"

"Better than adjusting. He actually sounds like Zack again. Tomorrow will only mark a week that he's been there, and he sounds better than he's sounded since he got back."

"That's wonderful! You and your sister must be thrilled. What an answer to prayer."

"That it is." He contemplated that thought for a moment as the gravity of what could have happened to Zack hit him. "That is exactly what it is. Zack could have been one of those suicide statistics. Now he's talking about playing basketball on his prosthetic leg when he gets home. He even thinks he's going to beat me. Fat chance." He laughed as he felt the release of months of worry about Zack. "He's going to therapy groups and doing some kind of tapping thing that sounded weird but he likes, and even a prayer group, and said he's figuring out some of what's been triggering him lately."

Bella came around the counter and hugged him. "I'm so happy for him – and you."

She felt good in his arms, and he didn't want to let her go. In fact, he didn't. He just leaned back and looked into her eyes; he could look into those blue pools forever. When the store phone rang, it sounded to him like it was behind a thick wall. On the third ring, he let her go and reached for the phone.

He looked at her with a crooked grin. "How did I get so distracted?"

She giggled as she said, "Sorry, boss."

"I'm not."

She blushed, then her face fell and she walked quickly toward the back of the store. He wasn't sure what had happened, but would find out as soon as he could get off the phone.

When he finished taking the phone order, Bella was nowhere to be found. He looked around the store, and finally found her in the office, hunched over her phone and texting frantically.

"Everything okay?"

She jumped at the sound of his voice, but quickly regained her composure. "It will be; it's just some leftover business in Dallas that I'm trying to get finished with. My attorney assured me that it will be done by Saturday." She gave him a warm smile and touched his arm as she started to pass him.

He didn't want to lose his opportunity or his nerve, and he reached out and pulled her back toward him. She took her place back in his arms as if she'd been there a thousand times before.

"Bella, I know it's a few days away, but can I take you out to breakfast before church on Sunday? I have to open the store right after, and since my only other employee right now is you, it's kind of hard to schedule a regular date." He found himself grinning at the thought of having an actual date with her, even over breakfast.

Her smile sent his heart racing.

"I would love to go on a breakfast date with you. A breakfast and church date sounds even better than a regular one."

Chapter 33

Bella sang along with the radio as she drove to work on Friday. She was having the time of her life helping in the store. That had a lot to do with Mitch, now that she had found out that rather than the ogre she initially thought he was, he was a thoroughly decent and kind man who she enjoyed spending time with. He was even letting her try things with displays and placement; she wasn't used to men outside her work in marketing taking her ideas seriously or even caring if she had a brain in her head, and it was a nice change.

Her worlds had always been separate, and it made her feel like she herself was separate. When she worked for the marketing firm, they valued her ideas and creativity, but they didn't give her the chance to work on some campaigns that she wanted to dig her hands into because they thought it didn't fit with her last name and country club membership. Her family and husband had *only* been interested in her ability to fit into the country club, show manners, and throw a party for people like them. Harrison only 'let' her work because she was able to do all that he demanded of her as well. She hadn't realized until she left Texas how exhausted she was from juggling two separate existences. Spending time working in the hardware store and exploring Summit County seemed to get her creative juices flowing again, and she was even enjoying working on her website and putting together proposals and marketing packages for a couple of smaller companies that had contacted her about doing some contract work.

She felt like she was coming alive again – or maybe for the first time. The one thing that was missing was the last piece of freedom from her old life. Harrison still hadn't signed the divorce papers, but had conveyed through his attorney that everything would be done by Saturday. She could wait one more day for him to follow through on a promise, but since that was not his strong suit, she was prepared to make another phone call after work if she hadn't heard confirmation from her attorney by then.

Harrison would be more likely to be alone and willing to have an honest conversation on a Saturday when he wasn't at the office or the club, and she was not going to be a part of his games any more. Once she got things settled with him, she could move forward with the rest of her life, including with Mitch. She still hadn't told him the details of her situation and wanted to be able to say that the divorce was in process before she went into it. If all went well, that would be the case by their Sunday breakfast date.

When she arrived at the hardware store, the parking lot was empty and there was no sign of Mitch. The store wasn't set to open for another half hour, but he was usually there at least an hour before opening. As she walked into the store and started making the coffee, she heard an unfamiliar rumbling outside. She opened the back door and her breath caught when she saw him climbing off a motorcycle with a huge grin on his face. When their eyes met, she felt a tingle in every cell and found herself matching his grin.

"You have a motorcycle?"

"Of course."

She imagined what it would be like to ride on one, with the wind rushing by. "Wow, I've never even been on one, and you have one of your own. I don't mind admitting that I'm a little jealous."

"You've never been on one?" He looked incredulous, as if the only people who hadn't ridden on motorcycles were those who lived in caves. Country clubs were their own kind of sheltered caves, so there were a lot of experiences she had missed out on. "Don't move."

He strode into the store while she examined the bike, loving the smooth feel of it and imagining riding down a country road. He appeared at her side seemingly within seconds with another helmet and handed it to her.

"We need to take care of this 'never been on a motorcycle' problem of yours."

"What about the store?"

"This is an emergency." He helped her strap the helmet on. "Plus, we'll just take a quick ride and be back in time to open it." He got on the bike in one smooth step and gestured for her to climb on behind him.

She fumbled a bit, but got on the seat, trying to figure out how to balance and not get too close to him. She looked around for handles.

"What do I hold onto?"

"Me."

It was a good thing that he'd turned his head after saying that so that he didn't see her cheeks suddenly turn red.

∞∞∞

The ride was short but glorious as he took her down a road that ran along a river and passed several farms. It was exactly the type of road motorcycles were made for, as far as she could tell. The feel of the wind rushing by was even better than she had imagined and she wished they could just keep going.

She didn't bother denying to herself how much she enjoyed having a reason to sit close and hold onto him. She was disappointed when the ride had to end, but it was tempered when Mitch said they could go on another, longer ride soon.

"That was a great way to start the day. Thank you for the ride."

"The first ride of the season is always the best. It was nice sharing it with you." His smile was even bigger after spending time on the bike, and it was nice to see him fully relaxing. Now that his nephew was on his way back to himself, Mitch seemed like he didn't have a care in the world.

Chapter 34

M itch couldn't take the smile off his face. The first day with the bike out of storage was always a good day, but being able to play hooky for a few minutes and take Bella out for a ride was icing on the cake. He was looking forward to taking her on a real ride, but that would have to wait for a couple of days.

Between getting to her place in the morning so he could finish what he'd started before he sliced his hand up, working at the store, and fixing Cynthia's washing machine after work, Saturday was off the table. Since their Sunday morning date would be followed by church, she probably wouldn't want to have helmet head to start the day. He comforted himself with the idea that maybe they could go Sunday after closing the store, and thought about places around Summit County that he wanted to show her.

Having her work with him at the store turned out to be a good business move and a lot of fun; she was a hard worker and good company. Now that he had asked her out, he didn't have to pretend that he wasn't enjoying being around her as much as he was. It was nice to feel so free with her.

He wished the next day was Sunday so that he didn't have to wait for their date, but told himself he could manage another thirty-six hours. The next day would fly by, anyway.

∞∞∞

The next morning, Mitch was finally feeling back to his competent self as he replaced the old pipes; he was almost able to use his hand normally now that it was healing and protected by a thick glove. It took focus to keep his mind on the pipes and not on the lady who lived there. Even though she had left to open the store, she was quite a distraction. He had to admit that it felt good to let his guard down with her. He made quick work out of the job and was about to start on the last pipe when a knock sounded at the door.

When he opened the door, he was surprised to see an overly-groomed man in a suit that looked like it cost more than his own truck holding a large bouquet of red roses.

"Can I help you?"

The man gave a polite but condescending smile as he looked past Mitch. "I'm looking for Isabella Langston."

Who? Bella? Who is this guy? Something about the man didn't sit well with Mitch, and it wasn't just the haughty tone or the way he said *Isabella*.

"She's not here right now. Can I tell her who stopped by?"

"I'm her husband; I'll wait."

Mitch felt like he'd been sucker-punched as the air left his lungs. He was so stunned by the word 'husband' that he didn't stop the man when he stepped past him into the small living room.

The man must have read Mitch's shock, and added, "I'm here to surprise her and take her home earlier than planned."

The way he smiled at Mitch made his skin crawl. He couldn't get out of there fast enough.

He forced his voice to stay steady. "I was just finishing up; I'll go tell her you're here."

The man – the *husband* – didn't look in Mitch's direction as he said, "Thank you" and held out a twenty-dollar bill toward him. Mitch ignored it and resisted the urge to swat it out of his hand as he walked past him and out the door.

His chest was tight and he had to remind himself to breathe as he made his way quickly down the stairs. His military training had come in handy for situations when he needed to hold his temper.

Once he got on the road, he was glad he was alone and no one could see his humiliation. "*Husband!* Funny, she didn't mention that."

Gripping the steering wheel only made his hand hurt worse, but the physical pain was almost comforting in a weird way. At least it distracted him momentarily from the hurt inside that was constricting his chest. "I can't believe I fell for another woman who toys with men. How could I have been so *stupid*!?"

The memories of Paula's betrayal came flooding back to him. When she made a fool of him, he made a vow to himself that it would never happen again. He had kept it from happening for years by staying away from women and pouring his energy into his business, family, and friends, and thought he might be able to trust his gut by now. Bella had seemed different, but it appeared that *Isabella* was cut from the same cloth as Paula.

By the time he got to the hardware store, his anger was boiling over, fueled by the pain that he was determined not to let her or anyone else see. He knew he needed to keep his words to a minimum and get away from her as fast as he could.

Chapter 35

I t surprised Bella to hear Mitch come through the back door in the afternoon.

"Wow, your hand really *is* working again. How did you finish so–" She stopped in her tracks when she saw the fire in his eyes; it made the first day they met seem like a day at the beach.

"Your workday is done."

"Mitch, what's wrong? What happened?" She started to move toward him, but he held up his hand.

"Go home, *Isabella*. Your husband is waiting."

"*What!?*"

"You heard me."

No! "Mitch, it's not what you think."

"It's none of my business. Don't forget to write down your hours and give me an address to send your check to before you leave." Mitch stormed into his office and slammed the door.

Harrison. How dare he?

Bella paced outside Mitch's office, fuming but wanting to explain herself and her situation. When he didn't come out, she realized he was waiting for her to leave. Her hands were shaking and she fought tears as she picked up her coat and purse and walked out the door.

She was livid as she drove back to the apartment. She wasn't sure who she was angrier at – Harrison for showing up and trying to poison her new life, or her mother for telling him where to find her.

This is what he meant by everything being done by Saturday!? Clearly, his idea of everything being done and mine are completely different, just like our ideas about everything else.

When she walked in the door, Harrison was sitting on *her* chair, which he had moved from its odd but perfect angle, with her suitcase next to him. It took him a moment to recognize her with her new look, and his jaw dropped.

"What did you do to your hai– What is that you're wearing?" Displeasure filled his tone.

"It's called a sweatshirt, Harrison; it's something normal people wear."

It looked like it took everything in him to switch gears and he turned on his most charming – and manipulative – smile.

"I'm sorry, darling. You just took me by surprise with your – whatever you call this." He waved his hand at her hair and clothing as he stood. When he took a step toward her with his arms out, she sidestepped him and glared at him.

"What are you doing here, Harrison?" She could barely contain her fury, and barely wanted to.

He straightened himself and held his smile. "I've come to give you another chance. I know we've had a misunderstanding, but it's not too late to come back. No one knows you've gone on this little . . ." he paused dramatically as he looked around the room with disdain, "camping vacation, and they don't need to find out."

"*Vacation*? I left you, Harrison. I filed for divorce, moved out of your house and your state, and started a new life. This is not a vacation, and I'm not going back." She stood firmly, hands on her hips, and refused to look away. "You made it sound like you were signing the papers. For once you need to follow through on your word."

"Isabella, be rational. We're not getting divorced. We have something special, and you love me. You're the one who always says marriage is forever."

"And you're the one who killed the marriage with your dating life."

"*Darling*, you know you're the only woman I love. Those dalliances mean nothing. Now come home with me and we'll let bygones be bygones." He was pouring the charm on even thicker, but she could see the strain was getting to him.

If the circumstances were different, she would have found it funny. As it was, she was too furious to be amused by anything.

"It's over and you need to leave." She met his eye squarely.

When he didn't get his way, his tone changed and he sounded like a father chastising a rebellious child. "Isabella, I've had enough of this. You've had your fun and made your point, running away like a child, but now it's time to face up to your responsibilities. Come home with me now and we'll forget this ever happened."

"I *am* home, and I want you to leave."

His eyes narrowed and brows lowered. She had never seen him look like that, and it unnerved her.

"You are trying my patience, and you have a very small window of opportunity. You need to come to your senses and come home with me." As he paused for effect, she wondered if he noticed that he used her mother's wording. "Don't think for a minute that there won't be someone ready to take your place."

She couldn't help but give a sarcastic laugh. "Women have *been* taking my place, Harrison. That was part of the problem. I'm not going with you now or ever. You need to leave." She pointed toward the door.

Bella had never seen him angry, and His eyes took on an intensity that gave her chills as he grabbed her suitcase with one hand and her arm with the other and started to pull her toward the door.

"We're going home. *Now.*"

Chapter 36

Mitch couldn't just sit in the store, and there were no customers anyway. Everywhere he looked, he saw changes that either Bella had made herself or they had made together. If he didn't get out of there soon, he thought he might explode.

He realized he had left his tool box at Bella's in his haste to leave, and needed it to fix Cynthia's washing machine that night.

He looked at the clock. *She's probably gone by now, on her way back to Dallas and laughing with her husband about her adventure living among the simple folk in the small town.*

Since he still had the key to the apartment, he locked the store and drove over there. When he arrived, the rental car was still in the driveway. He wanted to turn around and leave to avoid seeing Bella with her husband, but the thought of not letting Cynthia down propelled him forward. Nancy's car was there, too, so he decided to go talk to her for a few minutes while he waited for Bella to leave. He forced his gaze away from the direction of the apartment as he walked up the steps toward the house. As he neared the apartment, he heard a menacing tone in the man's voice. It put him on alert and shoved his personal feelings aside.

When he heard Bella's voice quiver in fear as she told the man to get his hands off of her, his instincts kicked in and he flew through the door. He saw relief on her face as he put himself between them and the husband took a step back.

The husband looked him square in the eye. "This doesn't concern you."

Mitch held his ground, glad that he had an inch and about twenty-five pounds on him. "The lady asked you to leave."

The husband smirked at Mitch, then looked past him to Bella with contempt in his eyes. "Is this what's been going on here? You've been cavorting with the *help*? You're better than that, Isabella."

He started toward the door and turned back to face her again. "You've got twenty-four hours. I suggest you think long and hard about what you're doing."

Mitch held his position until he heard the car leave.

Bella's voice was almost a whisper behind him. "Thank you, Mitch."

Mitch locked the door and looked out the windows to make sure the car had continued down the street. "Is he going to come back? You need to be somewhere safe."

"I don't think so. I don't know. I've never seen him like that before." She rubbed her arm.

"You shouldn't take any chances. Pack a bag, and I'll take you to the Ferrytown."

"Okay."

She seemed to go into auto-pilot, something he'd seen when he'd had to get Cynthia and Zack out of the same type of situation many years before. Bella put some clothes from the suitcase into a bag and quietly followed him out the door.

When they got in the truck, he called Wyatt to ask him to keep an eye out for the rental car while he was on patrol near the Ferrytown Motel. Wyatt suggested he encourage Bella to go down to the police station and make a report, but when she overheard him say it she just shook her head.

Mitch kept an eye on the rearview mirror and took a long, indirect route to the Ferrytown Motel to make sure they weren't being followed. He drove in silence as he scanned the area for any signs of the rental car.

"Mitch, thank you. I'm sorry for what he said about you. He can be–"

"Bella," he cut her off, keeping his eyes far from her. "Let's not do this. I'm just making sure you're safe and I'll be on my way."

"I'm sorry. I owe you an explanation."

He had no use for explanations or excuses; he was protecting a woman from a threatening man, and that was it. He still worked to contain his fury, both at her and at himself for being duped again.

"Your marriage is none of my business."

"It's not what it looks like. I told you I left my marriage."

"You should have told him." His eyes scanned every direction but hers.

"I *did* tell him. I had him served with divorce papers well before I left Dallas. The only reason he can still call himself my husband is that he hasn't signed them. Did that look like a marriage to you back there?"

It wasn't easy hearing the pain in her voice, but since he had nothing to say, he remained silent. He breathed a sigh of relief when they arrived at the Ferrytown Motel. He wanted to be far from her and couldn't bear to look at her. As she got out of the truck, he stared out his window and wished he was anywhere but there.

Chapter 37

Bella fought tears as she looked around the tiny motel room, missing her perfect little apartment and feeling as alone as she had ever felt. Her phone buzzed, and she was relieved to see that this time it was Emily calling, not her mother, like every other call in the last hour.

"Are you okay? Can I come over?"

"You talked to Mitch?"

"He thought you could use a friend."

The word 'friend' unleashed the tears that Bella had tried so hard to stifle. They were choking her and she couldn't form the words she wanted to say.

"I'm on my way. What room are you in?"

When they came out, the words were barely more than a whisper. She somehow managed to say, "Five." As she hung up the phone, she sat on the bed and let the tears flow.

Emily arrived within twenty minutes and greeted her with a long hug and a thermos full of hot tea.

"Do you want to talk about it?"

Bella just nodded, unable to say anything, and walked over to sit on the bed.

Emily sat next to her and held her hand. "It's going to be okay. Take your time."

It took a minute to find words, but once she did, they came gushing out in a torrent. "I just can't believe Harrison came here. He thought he could charm me and then threaten me and I would go back with him. It only validated my decision to leave him and that life behind. He was awful to Mitch and now Mitch thinks I lied to him."

"What happened?"

Bella told her the story, from seeing the look of hurt and anger on Mitch's face when he stormed into the hardware store to Harrison's manipulations and threats to Mitch's rescue then coldness. While she was spilling her story out, her mother called three times. She ignored them all and wished she'd gotten a new number when she came to town. She only kept the phone on in case Mitch would call or text, and every time the phone rang and it was anyone but him, her heart sank further.

"Remember what I told you about this being a good place for healing? You're going to get over this and be okay. When I came to town, I was hurting and didn't trust men or my own judgment; I could only trust God. Now it doesn't even seem like that life before ever existed."

Bella just nodded, trying to grasp the hope and comfort that Emily was offering.

"It's not the old life that's got you down, is it? When I walked in here, you were distraught, but not about your husband or your marriage. This is more about Mitch, isn't it?"

The next wave of tears surprised Bella; she didn't think she had any more in her until she heard Mitch's name. "I don't think he's ever going to speak to me again. He wouldn't even look at me in the car when he brought me here. I can't believe Harrison even took Mitch from me."

Emily put her arm around her. "When he called me to tell me what happened, I could hear the hurt in his voice. If he didn't care about you, he wouldn't be hurting. Give him some time to cool down and maybe you can talk it out. I don't know what happened to him, but I know he's been hurt before. Joe and I are living proof that people who have been hurt in the past can find happiness again." Just then, Emily's phone rang and she smiled. "Speak of the devil."

As she spoke with Joe, Bella took comfort from her face and voice. *It is possible to move on. I just want to move on* with *Mitch, not* from *him.*

"Are you hungry?"

Bella nodded enthusiastically.

"Yes, we would love that ... No way, no girl food. We need pizza, extra cheesy pizza. Thanks, honey. You're the best."

She hung up the phone and smiled. "Food delivery is on the way. He's glad you're okay."

Bella's phone buzzed again and she rolled her eyes as she held it up to show Emily that it was her mother calling. "She's been calling since I was in the truck with Mitch. I'm sure Harrison called her before he was even out of my driveway, and now she's calling to tell me what a terrible mistake I'm making and remind me what a disappointment I am to her."

Emily grinned. "Want me to show you how to send her calls straight to voice mail?"

"Oh, yes, please!" She felt like she'd just reclaimed her phone when she set calls from her mother and Harrison to both go to voice mail. Her father and sister didn't call her, so she didn't need to bother with them.

She washed her face, and by the time Joe got there to drop off the pizza and a friendly hug, she was feeling a bit better.

∞∞∞

Hours later, Bella's stomach was full from the pizza they had gorged themselves on and her heart was full from having a friend who was willing to sit and listen to her all evening.

"That pizza hit the spot." She picked up Emily's coat and handed it to her. "Thank you again for coming. You're a good friend."

"I can stay with you tonight if you want me to."

"No, I'll be okay. Mitch asked a sheriff's deputy he knows to be on the lookout for the rental car just in case, so it will be fine."

Emily looked out the window as she was putting her coat on and smiled. "Wyatt isn't the only one on the lookout tonight."

Bella walked over to the window. When she saw Mitch's truck in the parking lot, her breath caught.

"Mitch is more a man of action than words, and his actions say he cares about you. You still have a chance."

"Let's hope. Thanks again for everything, Emily." She hugged her friend goodbye and decided to go outside and try to talk to Mitch.

Chapter 38

Mitch finished off his lukewarm coffee and tried to focus on watching for the rental car and keeping his mind clear. When he saw Bella come out of the motel room with a box of pizza in one hand and a cup of something that looked hot in the other, his chest clenched. He put down his window and looked at her for the first time since her husband showed up, then immediately regretted it.

"I brought you some stakeout food." She handed it through the window and asked, "May I sit in here with you for a minute?"

He nodded and unlocked the doors. He took a deep breath and asked God to help him as she got into the car.

"Thank you for calling Emily. I'm so used to not having friends around that it didn't occur to me that I could do that. I really needed a friend."

He just nodded, not knowing what to say.

"Actually, thank you for everything you did today." She fidgeted with her coat sleeve. "I get the feeling this wasn't the first time you helped someone out of a situation like that."

"No, it wasn't." Mitch looked off into the distance and tried not to remember Cynthia's frightened eyes the night he stood between her and Zack's father. Mitch was only a teenager at the time, but the fear he saw in Cynthia and Zack fueled his courage. Fortunately, Cynthia got out and stayed out of the relationship.

He hoped Bella would make as wise a choice as his brave sister had. "Hopefully today was the last time."

"I hope so, too." Her voice was tentative as she asked, "May I tell you my story while you eat your pizza?"

"It's really not my business what you do with your life, Bella."

"I want you to know. Maybe you'll understand."

"Okay." He tried focusing more on the pizza than her closeness in the truck.

"I'll start at the beginning, if you don't mind." She cleared her throat. "Growing up in my family, there were certain expectations. I never met most of them. I got good grades and stayed out of trouble, but those were only the basics and barely counted."

He couldn't help but remember the times his parents praised his efforts and character and celebrated his accomplishments as she continued. "I was never like my parents and my sister, and I never fit in with the country clubs or dinner parties, or with *them*, for that matter. I'm probably the only person in history whose act of rebellion was going to youth groups instead of playing golf or tennis at the club." She laughed nervously. "We moved around every couple of years because of my father's job, so I don't have friends who I've known since childhood like you have with Joe and the other people I've seen you with around here."

Her voice softened and he heard the sadness as she described a completely different existence than he had. "I never had any deep friendships until I met my best friend in college. The only person I've known longer than her is Harrison. He was one of the few constants in my life, and is the only non-family member I've known since I was a child. Since our families were close, it was always sort of assumed that he and I would be together."

Mitch wanted to interrupt to ask her to just get to the part where she said she was going back to Dallas so he could wish her a good life and go get some sleep. She sounded like she needed to tell her story, though, so he kept listening as she continued.

"The first time I ever remember seeing approval on my parents' faces was the day Harrison and I got engaged. When we got married, I hoped it would be a good marriage, one that would last forever. I had thought that he felt as stifled by that life as I had growing up and that we would break free of it together, but I couldn't have been more wrong." The sadness in her voice only deepened as she described her broken dreams. "He actually loved it and planned to walk in our parents' footsteps, but had never let on when I talked about how much I hated it. I guess he figured I would just fall in step when we got married."

She fumbled with her sleeve again while she spoke. "He never treated me poorly or acted the way you saw him today. He never used threats or put his hands on me. Manipulation and charm were more his style."

He could see out of the corner of his eye that she was looking directly at him, maybe to assure him that what she was saying was true. Even though he was losing his appetite more with each word she spoke, the pizza gave him the needed excuse not to look at her.

"I soon found that the way to make him happy was to wear the designer clothes that he insisted on buying for me – even though I hated them – and to be the perfect hostess in our cold showplace of a home. He didn't care that I was smart or good at my career or a decent human being. He wanted a wife who could fit in at the club and throw a good party. Since I was trained in that world just like he was, I could do that. Even though we were completely different, I believe marriage is sacred and is supposed to be forever, and I tried everything I could think of to make it better. I tried to be what he wanted, and I failed at it just like I failed at being what my parents wanted."

He was starting to wonder where this was going and shifted in his seat.

"When I first found out that he had a mistress, my best friend had just had a baby and I didn't want to dump that on her. I had no one else to talk to, so I went to my mother for support. I'm not sure why I thought that was a good idea, but I was desperate. When I told her she didn't act at all surprised, and she told me to grow up and stop believing in childish fantasies about happily-ever-after and fidelity. Her advice to me if I wanted a chance at having him to myself was to go on a diet, climb higher on the social ladder, and keep my mouth shut". Bella's voice grew soft. "Basically, her advice was to find a way to get better at not being myself."

Mitch couldn't believe what he was hearing; it was like something out of the soap operas his sisters used to watch when they were babysitting him. *How could a mother be so cruel?*

She took a deep breath as she seemed to be willing herself to continue. "I gave him another chance after he promised me that he had ended it and told me he loved me and that it meant nothing. I didn't realize until later that he had carefully avoided saying that it was wrong or he wouldn't do it again. He just said he would make things better and didn't want me to leave. Shock of shocks, it happened again, and I was done."

The determination he had witnessed in her started returning to her voice. "When I told my parents I was leaving Harrison, they acted as if I had just committed the worst offense possible. They've barely spoken to me since. My mother has to be the one who told Harrison where to find me, because other than my best friend, she's the only one I gave the address to. She's been calling me since you and I were driving away from the apartment, and I can assure you it's to remind me of the ways I've failed her. Nothing Harrison said this afternoon will compare to what she will say."

She paused and stared at him until he raised his head and looked at her. He wanted to look away, but couldn't do it.

"When I left Dallas and left Harrison, it was for good. I knew when I did it that I would likely be disowned by my family and so-called friends other than my best friend. I knew it and did it anyway because that life was killing me. I sold my designer clothes and pretentious car that Harrison loved, and left there with the few possessions I cared about to start life over in the one place I remembered feeling happy."

She pulled an old picture of two young girls in front of the "Welcome to Summit County" sign out of her pocket and handed it to Mitch. "I didn't even know where Summit County was; I had to Google it. When I moved here and started making friends and growing roots, I felt like myself again. And when I started getting to know you, I saw the possibilities for a different future and a real relationship." She looked at him apologetically. "I'm sorry I didn't tell you the full story about my marriage. I wasn't trying to deceive you. I just assumed there would be time and that by the time I could tell you about it, the legal proceedings would be moving along."

He looked down to avoid her stare as she waited for him to respond. His thoughts were nowhere near collected and he was taking in everything she was telling him while trying not to let his guard down.

Her voice started to tremble a bit as she continued. "I was crushed by how Harrison treated you in the apartment. You don't deserve to be spoken to or about like that. The time I've spent with you has been wonderful and–" The resolve she'd shown so far in telling her story started to crumble before his eyes as she talked about the scene in the apartment earlier, and it took every bit of his own resolve to stay still and listen.

She paused and looked like she couldn't go on, but took a breath and continued with tears in her eyes. "I know you hate me right now, but I just wanted you to know how things got to this point and why I was married to the man you saw at his worst today. You now know more about me and my life than 99% of the people I know."

He had no point of reference for how he was feeling or what he should do. The lump in his throat worked with the tightness in his chest to render him unable to speak. He couldn't look at her and hold it together, so he found himself staring at the empty pizza box.

As she quietly got out of the truck and walked back to her room without looking back, he felt like he was paralyzed. A part of him wanted to call her back to the truck or to follow her, but he couldn't make his mouth or his legs move.

Chapter 39

Bella woke up early the next morning feeling disoriented and confused. As she rubbed her eyes and slowly forced herself to sit upright, she quickly remembered why she was back at the Ferrytown Motel and what had happened the day before. She was thankful for the coffeemaker in the room and hoped it would help the pounding in her head once she could motivate herself to actually use it.

When she remembered that it was Sunday and that it was supposed to be the day of her breakfast date with Mitch, her head pounded more and she felt a new batch of tears threaten. She debated about whether or not she should go to church while she took a long shower and tried to wash the previous day's events away.

After getting dressed, she sat on the bed and stared into space as she replayed the previous day in her head. She lost track of time and jumped when she heard light tapping on the door. When she peeked out the window and saw Mitch standing there with a bag from the bakery and two large coffees, she thought she was dreaming.

Relief flooded her when she opened the door and saw that he was really standing there. "Mitch! Would you like to come in?"

As he handed one of the coffees and the bag of donuts to her while walking past her, she realized he was still in the clothes he was wearing the day before and must have spent all night in the parking lot. He looked like he was focused on something and she wasn't sure what to say.

"You told me your story last night, and I think it's time to tell you mine today." He looked around, and since the only other option was the bed, sat on the edge of the dresser.

"When I joined the Army, I planned to be career. I knew what that meant for having a home life, but serving my country felt like a calling to me. I met a girl on base whose father was a colonel, and when we started dating and getting serious, I thought it was a sign that I could have the career and the home life because she *got* it." He took a sip of his coffee and kept his gaze on the floor. "We were together for a year before I had a deployment, and I asked her to marry me before I left, even though something in my gut said to wait. We talked on the phone and emailed the whole time I was gone and everything seemed fine, so I chalked the gut feeling up to jitters. I didn't tell her when I was coming home because I wanted to surprise her."

Bella braced herself for what was coming. If this story had a happy ending, he wouldn't be here telling it to her.

"The short version is that I came home from a fifteen-month deployment to a very pregnant fiancée."

She gasped. "Oh, Mitch." *How could someone do that to him?*

"My supposed friends – the people I had to trust my life to on the battlefield – knew and didn't tell me. They all said no one told me because they didn't want me to be distracted while I was in a war zone. The guy she was messing around with was someone I had considered a friend." He shook his head as if to try to clear it. "When that happened, I decided I was done with women and with soldiers and was coming back to Hideaway when my four years were up. My friends in Hideaway never would have kept a secret like that from me or let me be humiliated like that."

He finally looked her in the eye. "When your husband showed

up, it felt like that all over again. Actually, it was worse, because I feel completely different when I'm with you than I ever did when I was with her. It sent me into a tailspin and I didn't know how to get out of it, or if I wanted to try. I still don't."

She didn't know what to say, but found herself walking to where he was sitting on the edge of the dresser and wrapping her arms around him. She just held him for a moment before speaking. "I'm so sorry, Mitch. I'm so sorry I gave you reason to think I was like that."

It seemed like an eternity before he put his arms around her, but when he did, he held her so tightly she thought he might not let her go. She knew she didn't want him to and held him just as tightly.

Bella stepped back and loosened the embrace after a few moments. "So what do we do now? Can we start over?"

He half-smiled. "You mean with me yelling at you about messing up my store and you glaring at me for being late to your apartment?"

"Something like that, but maybe totally different."

He looked serious as he dropped his hands from her waist. "I still don't date married women, Bella. Is there something you can do about that?"

"Actually, I have an idea about that." She handed him her phone and pulled up the sleeve of her shirt to reveal the black and purple marks left by Harrison's hand. Mitch's eyes widened, then he looked like he could rip Harrison apart limb by limb.

"He did me a favor when he crossed the line and did this. Will you take a picture of it?"

He took pictures from different angles, and Bella sent some to Harrison with a message: "Sign the divorce papers and get them to my attorney's office by 1pm my time today or these pictures go to the police here and the newspapers there."

Satisfied, she looked back at him with a tentative smile. "How do you feel about dating women whose divorce papers are signed and filed?"

"I think I can manage that when that happens." He returned the smile, then looked at his watch. "In the meantime, since we're not going on a breakfast date this morning, let's get you home and finish that last pipe before church. I need to open the store as soon as church gets out and I think I accidentally fired my best employee yesterday."

"Was that also your only employee?"

He slapped his hand to his head. "I've got to get better at running a business."

She offered him one of the donuts on a napkin. "Maybe the employee will come back if you're nice and promise a weekly donut run."

Chapter 40

A few days later, Mitch finished unpacking the boxes of potting soil and loading them on the shelves in record time. He turned when the bells on the front door jingled and a smiling Bella walked in to start her shift.

"Wow, that's very handy, having the potting soil right there. Whoever gave you such an idea?"

He grinned at her. "Some big-city smarty pants marketing genius."

Joe walked in right behind Bella. "Ahh, just the two people I wanted to see. I'm on a mission from Emily."

"Oh? Is that like a mission from God?" He tried to do his best Blues Brothers impression, but fell a bit short.

Joe looked intently at Mitch. "Four days from our wedding, it's pretty close. She's working on the seating chart for the reception and, in her words, since you haven't pulled the trigger and invited Bella to be your plus one, she's rescinding your plus one and inviting Bella herself."

He turned and handed an invitation to Bella, who squealed with delight and accepted. She turned to Mitch and sang, "Ha ha, you can't get away from me now."

"I have no intention of getting away from you." She blushed as she caught the look in his eyes. He wished he could have asked her to the wedding himself, but until something changed in her marital situation, he was determined to continue to wait.

Bella's text notification sounded just as Joe left the store. She held the phone close and squinted at the screen as if she was trying to decipher what it said. She walked closer to where he was standing by the displays and turned it toward him.

"Can you read what that says? Something about papers filed and 60-day waiting period started? Is that what that says?" She looked up at him with a big grin and a twinkle in her eye.

His own grin and twinkle appeared immediately and matched hers as he took a step closer to her. "Hmm, filed, huh? I guess we get to schedule that date now."

"Too bad you don't have a plus one for a wedding to offer. It doesn't count now that I've been invited on my own merits."

"I'm not waiting four more days, and I think I just heard the boss saying something about closing the store a little early tonight. Do you have plans for dinner?"

"I think my plans just changed."

He reached out and pulled her close, careful not to touch her still-healing arm.

"How do you feel about kissing before the first date?" He cupped her cheek gently with his free hand as he looked into her eyes.

She just smiled and turned her lips up toward his; he could feel the pounding in his chest as he met them with his own. As he got lost in the kiss, he felt his fears and the walls in his heart melt away. The woman who had once been so dangerous to him was now his refuge.

As they sank further into their embrace, he felt his strength leave him; he stepped back to shore up his stance and felt his foot hit something. A crashing sound startled them both and broke the kiss. They turned to see the gardening display scattering all over the front of the store.

Bella giggled. "You can just put that everywhere. Now that the boss is cavorting with the help, anything goes around here."

Dear Reader,

Hopefully if you've read this far, you enjoyed the book! I know you're busy and have other things (and books!) clamoring for your time and attention, and I hope this story brought a little brightness into your day. Mitch and Bella will continue to pop up in smaller roles in other books in the series and you can see their story progress along in the background while other residents of Summit County take center stage.

If you would like to leave a review on Amazon so that other readers can be introduced to this book, I would be so grateful. If having to leave a full review is just too much (I get it - they take precious time that could be spent reading!), but you'd like to leave a rating on Goodreads, you can do that, too!

See you in Summit County,

Katherine

Summit County Series, Book 6

You can never go back to your first love – or can you?

Brianna Callahan is known for her huge heart, unwavering dedication to those she loves, and tendency to dump great boyfriends without cause. Even while she encourages her friends and family to be vulnerable and accept love, she has impenetrable walls built around her own heart, thanks to a heartbreak from long ago.

Garrett Ryan is thought to be a wanderer who doesn't want to grow up and get his life together. He lets people think what they want and goes about his business serving God and helping people all over the world. As for his own heartbreak from years gone by, he refuses to entertain either the questions or the answers he never understood.

When a family emergency forces Garrett to come to the one place in the world he's tried to avoid – home – the two must come face to face with the youthful love that never died and the pain they still carry. But first, they must find a way to be in the same room without throttling each other.

Coming soon to Amazon in Kindle and Paperback formats!

About the Author

Katherine Karrol is both a fan and an author of lighthearted, sweet, clean Christian romance stories. Because she does not possess the ability or desire to put a good book down and generally reads them in one sitting, she writes books that can be read in the same way.

Her books are meant to entertain and even possibly inspire the reader to take chances, trust God, and laugh at life. The people she interacts with in her professional life have absolutely no idea that she writes these books, so by reading this, you agree to keep her secret.

If you would like to contact her to share your favorite character or share who you were picturing as you were reading, you can follow her on Goodreads, Facebook, Twitter, and Instagram, or email her at KatherineKarrol@gmail.com.

About the Summit County Series

The Summit County Series is a group of standalone books that can be read individually, but those who read all of them in order will get a little extra something out of them as they see the characters and stories they've read about previously continue and will get glimpses of characters that may be featured in future books. The series is set in a small county in Northern Michigan, where everyone knows everyone else, so the same characters and places make cameos and sometimes show up in significant roles in multiple books.

This series is near and dear to the author's heart because she spends as much time as possible in places that look an awful lot like the places in Summit County. She is certain that the people who know her and/or live in the area that inspired Summit County will think characters and situations are based on them or their neighbors (or even on her) and she assures them that they are not. The characters and stories are merely figments of her overly active imagination. Well, except for Jesus. He's totally real.

The books are available on Amazon in both paperback and Kindle formats.

.

Made in the USA
Lexington, KY
26 July 2019